"I came to see you, not your father."

Carl's lazy, heavy-lidded eyes challenged her as he spoke. Morgan felt as if the breath had momentarily been squeezed from her lungs, and she was suddenly terrified that he might hear the erratic beat of her heart.

"You came to see me?" she asked huskily.

"You find that hard to believe?"

Shaking, she clutched the sides of the recliner in an effort to hide the fact. "Why should you want to see me?"

"You're a very pretty lady, and when I saw you yesterday, I said to myself, 'Now here's someone I'd like to know better.'"

"What gave you the idea I'd feel the same way about you?" Morgan demanded stiffly.

"I'm seldom wrong," he said simply.

YVONNE WHITTAL

web of silk

Harlequin Books

TORONTO • NEW YORK • LOS ANGELES • LONDON
AMSTERDAM • PARIS • SYDNEY • HAMBURG
STOCKHOLM • ATHENS • TOKYO • MILAN

Harlequin Presents first edition March 1983
ISBN 0-373-10582-7

Original hardcover edition published in 1982
by Mills & Boon Limited

CHAPTER ONE

A WARM, sunny day in midwinter was nothing strange in Rossmere, which nestled amongst the hills ninety kilometres north of Pretoria, but the moment the sun dipped behind those hills the temperature dropped several degrees below zero, and for this reason alone Morgan Field was determined to soak up every scrap of warmth that Saturday afternoon on the terrace of her father's home.

She lay back on the cane recliner, and her thick dark lashes fanned her cheeks when she closed her eyes. Her titian-coloured hair lay spread out in an aureole about her head against the floral cushions, and her small, thrusting breasts rose and fell gently beneath the green silk blouse. Below the hem of her white woollen skirt one shapely calf and ankle was exposed to the sun, while her right leg was encased in a heavy plaster cast from below the knee down to just above the toes. The cast was an uncomfortable reminder of how she had allowed herself to be coerced into going horse-riding. The tetchy mare had thrown her after a few nerve-racking minutes, and she had been lucky to escape with nothing more serious than bruises and a broken leg.

Morgan felt pleasantly drowsy, and she must have dozed off for a while, but when she once again became aware of the birdsong around her, she had the uneasy feeling that she was being observed. She stirred, her lashes lifting to reveal eyes which were a mixture of grey and green beneath dark, winged brows, and her heart lurched violently when she found herself staring up into the bluest eyes she had ever seen. Those eyes belonged to a man whose hair was so fair it was almost white in the sunlight, and it contrasted heavily with the deeply tanned skin stretching across his strong features. His shoulders were broad beneath the perfectly tailored blue jacket, and his thumbs were hooked into the pockets of his grey corded pants which clung to lean hips and long, muscular legs. His jaw was square beneath the chiselled, frankly sensuous mouth, and he exuded a raw masculinity which reached out to her and left her incredibly aware of her own femininity.

Startled, and faintly amused at the feelings he aroused, a slow, spontaneous smile lifted the corners of her wide mouth. 'How long have you been standing there?'

'A few seconds, no more.' His voice was deep, velvety, and unmistakably American, but it was the teasing, almost mocking light in his eyes that captured her attention. 'I give you my word that you didn't snore.'

'I should hope not!' she laughed lightly, but her laugh had a curiously breathless sound to it which vaguely irritated her as she swung her legs off the recliner and reached for her crutches.

'Don't get up,' he ordered at once, thrusting his hand out towards her, and it was a nice hand with neatly clipped nails she noticed. 'I'm Carl Ziegler.'

'Morgan Field,' she responded politely.

His hand embraced hers. There was no other way to describe it, she decided. Others shook hands, or clasped, or gripped, but the touch of this man's hand was like an intimate embrace that sent a thousand little shock waves tripping across exposed nerve ends.

'I didn't know Andrew had a daughter.'

Morgan felt as if something had a stranglehold on her throat, but she was saved from making a suitable reply when her father stepped out on to the terrace at that precise moment.

'Carl,' he smiled at his visitor, and it needed only a quick glance to sum up the situation. 'I presume you two have introduced yourselves?'

'We have,' Carl Ziegler replied, his hand releasing Morgan's at last and allowing her to breathe a little easier.

'If you'll come this way then we can talk privately in the study,' Andrew Field suggested after an awkward pause, and Carl nodded before he turned to smile at Morgan in a way that succeeded in sending the blood skipping through her veins.

'You will excuse us, won't you, Miss Field?'

'Yes, of course,' she was surprised to hear herself reply in a pleasant yet deceptively calm voice.

The two men disappeared into the house and Morgan sat there wondering if she had not imagined her brief yet electrifying encounter with this man who called himself Carl Ziegler. No man had ever affected her in quite this way before. She was level-headed and sensible, and quite content with the way her life was progressing, but in the space of a few minutes he had made her aware of herself as a woman, soft and totally feminine, and quite suddenly unknown forces were clamouring for an outlet within her. It was disturbing, and more than a little frightening.

Who was he? What was he doing here in the small industrial town of Rossmere? She could not find the answer to these questions, but something warned her that this man could prove to be dangerous to her peace of mind.

Morgan levered herself up on to the crutches and entered the house laboriously. She was no longer in the right mood to enjoy the warmth and tranquillity of the terrace, but most of all she did not want to be around when Carl Ziegler left the house. He was the type of man she was certain she could take in small doses only, and the initial dose had been ample to leave her shaken beyond her understanding. She passed the study on her way to her room, and heard the word 'Triton' being mentioned behind the closed door, but she did not linger to hear more. It was a business discussion, that much was obvious, but exactly where Carl Ziegler fitted in she was curious to know.

The Triton Computer Company had put Rossmere on the map a number of years ago, and her father, Andrew Field, was one of the senior directors of a firm which was headed by a crusty old man named Randolph Hillier. More than that Morgan could not recall. She had never been all that interested in computers, and her father had seldom discussed his work, or those with whom he worked. When Andrew closed his office door behind him in the evenings, or at weekends, that was where it all remained, and it was totally unusual for him to have someone coming to his home to discuss anything connected with business. It was this realisation that made Morgan wonder once again what Carl Ziegler's connection was with the company.

That evening, while Morgan and her father were having their after-dinner coffee in front of the living-room fire, she could no longer contain her curiosity.

'Tell me about Carl Ziegler,' she said with as much

casualness as she could muster. 'Does he work for the Triton Company?'

'Carl Ziegler *is* the Triton Company,' her father informed her drily, and when he met her curious gaze he launched into a lengthy explanation which surprised her even more. 'When Randolph Hillier retired last year his nephew, Carl, came out from America at Randolph's request to take the chair. Hillier's decision to install Carl as president and chairman of the company caused a tremendous stir amongst the existing directors, but we have all had to admit that he's a genius with computers, and his business acumen is razor-sharp. No one can deny that the company has expanded under his guidance over the past months. Sales have risen to phenomenal heights, and bigger and better contracts have been coming our way.'

'So he has brain as well as brawn,' she remarked absently, and her father's face creased into an amused smile.

'The men most certainly appreciate his brain, but I have no doubt that the women are more interested in the brawn.'

'Is he a bit of a wolf?'

'He had a reputation, I believe, for changing his women more often than there are seasons in a year.'

'He's obviously of the opinion that variety adds spice to life,' she murmured, staring thoughtfully into the fire. 'Intriguing thought.'

'What did you think of him?' Andrew shot the question at her.

'I can't really say,' she frowned, being deliberately vague, but she recalled only too vividly her feelings when he had held her hand. 'I only met him briefly this afternoon, as you know.'

'Stay out of his way, Morgan. He's not your type.'

She glanced sharply at her father, taking in his dark hair which was greying so attractively at the temples, and the concern of his stiff youthful-looking features, then she laughed lightly.

'Good heavens, Daddy,' she protested. 'With this heavy cast on my leg I can't very well get *into* his way, now can I?'

'You know what I mean,' her father scowled. 'Don't encourage him, whatever you do.'

'I promise to wear my "Little Miss Prune" face the next time he calls,' she said, adding the action to her words.

'Be serious, Morgan,' he scowled, meeting her mischievous glance. 'I know you're old enough to do as you please, but do be careful where Carl Ziegler is concerned.'

'I didn't know that Randolph Hillier had relatives in America,' she remarked, deciding it was safer to steer the conversation on to firmer ground.

'Hillier's sister married an American. Carl was born here in South Africa, but when he was fifteen his parents went to America, and I suppose twenty years in that country was long enough for Carl to pick up their accent.'

That made him thirty-five, Morgan thought after a quick bout of mental arithmetic, and somehow, even though their discussion had ended there, she could not rid her mind of the man who had reminded her of a Viking god. He invaded her dreams that night, along with the warnings her father had issued, and when she awoke on Sunday morning she was of the same mind as her father. The less she saw of Carl Ziegler, the better for her, and she hoped that he would conduct all further business discussions with her father during company time, and on company premises.

Andrew Field went off to his usual game of golf that Sunday, and Morgan settled down with a book on the terrace. It was not often that she had the opportunity to catch up on her reading, but this enforced holiday had given her plenty of time to indulge in her favourite pastime. The enjoyment of it was beginning to pall slightly, but she nevertheless settled down with one of her favourites in the hope that she would become totally absorbed in it.

Morgan had been reading for more than an hour in the shade of the bougainvillea when a sleek silver Porsche purred up the circular drive and stopped just below the steps, and to her consternation Carl Ziegler got out of it and mounted the steps with lithe, easy strides. Morgan held her breath as she watched him approach her, and for some unaccountable reason there was a nervous fluttering in her breast as his potent masculinity reached out to her once more.

'Good morning,' he smiled, drawing up a chair and seating himself close to her.

'Good morning, Mr Ziegler,' she returned his greeting stiffly, setting aside her book and folding her hands rather primly in her lap.

'My friends call me Carl.'

In a beige lightweight suit and brown open-necked shirt, he looked absolutely devastating, but Morgan was determined to remain outwardly unimpressed. 'My association with you is too brief for me to think of you as a friend.'

'I make friends easily.'

'Do you?' she mocked him, while withdrawing mentally from the sensual attraction that emanated from him.

'I detect a certain reserve in your manner,' he remarked quietly, almost challengingly.

'I'm always reserved with strangers,' she lied, her voice a little huskier than usual.

'That wasn't the impression I got yesterday.'

'That was yesterday,' she walked unsuspectingly into the trap.

'I get it,' he smiled, and her bones seemed to melt at the sight of it despite the mockery curving his chiselled mouth. 'Your daddy has told you not to mess with the big bad wolf, and nice little girls like you usually do what their daddies tell them.'

'Nice little girls usually heed the warnings of their elders, but that should still leave them free to make up their own minds about something or someone,' she corrected him primly.

'And are you free to make up your own mind?'

She looked up into those lazy, heavy-lidded eyes, and said abruptly, 'I'm over twenty-one.'

'I bet you're making that up, and that you're not a day older than eighteen,' he laughed, displaying strong white teeth.

'Flattery will get you nowhere, Mr Ziegler.'

'Carl,' he corrected, and she found it unnerving that he should observe her so intently. 'How old are you?'

'A gentleman never questions a lady about her age,' she prevaricated mockingly.

'That's correct, ma'am, but I'm no gentleman, so I'll ask you again,' he said. 'How old are you?'

'I don't see that it's any business of yours,' she

replied with unusual haughtiness, 'but I'm twenty-four.'

'Nice age ... twenty-four,' he murmured, and she wished he would stop looking at her in that peculiarly intense fashion as if he was contemplating making a meal of her.

'If you were hoping to see my father, then I'm afraid you've missed him,' she said, hoping he would go away and leave her in peace. 'He usually plays golf on a Sunday.'

'I came to see you, not your father.'

Morgan felt as if the breath had momentarily been squeezed from her lungs, and she was suddenly terrified that he might hear the erratic beat of her heart. 'You came to see *me*?'

'You find that hard to believe?'

Her hands were suddenly shaking so much that she clutched the sides of the recliner in an effort to hide the fact. 'Why should you want to see me?'

'You're a very pretty lady, and when I saw you yesterday I said to myself, "Now here's someone I'd like to get to know better".'

'What gave you the idea that I would feel the same way about you?' she demanded stiffly.

'I'm seldom wrong about such things.'

Those very blue eyes flicked over her, challenging, razor-sharp, and missing nothing from the uncertain flutter of her hands to that frightened little pulse at the base of her throat. A triumphant little smile curved his sensuous mouth, and she felt her cheeks grow warm with embarrassment.

'Mr Ziegler——'

'Carl,' he interrupted urgently, leaning towards her

and trapping her within the aura of his disturbing masculinity. *'Say it!'*

Morgan stared up into his ruggedly handsome face. She saw the tiny laughter lines beneath his eyes, the bone-melting persuasiveness of his smile, and somehow she heard herself complying with the command he had given.

'Carl,' she said his name in her faintly husky voice.

'I knew it!' he announced abruptly, snapping his fingers and leaning back in the cane chair with a satisfied expression settling on his face.

'Knew what?' she questioned confusedly.

'I knew that when you said my name it would sound pleasantly different from the way anyone else said it.'

Their eyes met, and Morgan felt as if she were hovering on the brink of a deep ravine. 'I think you'd better go.'

'I can hear tea cups rattling inside,' he announced smoothly. 'You're going to invite me to stay and have tea with you, aren't you?'

'No, I'm not!' the words hovered on her lips, but she realised in time that this man was not only the president and chairman of Triton, but her father's senior, so she sighed and said resignedly, 'I suppose it would be impolite of me not to ask you to stay to tea.'

'And I accept your gracious invitation . . . Morgan.'

He was mocking her, but it was the sound of her name on his lips, more than anything else, that did strange things to her.

Paulina's arrival with the tea was a welcome diversion. It gave Morgan something to do, and time to gather her scattered wits about her, but even while she sat up to pour the tea she was intensely conscious of

Carl Ziegler's forceful presence. He was seated much too close to her for comfort, and one careless movement would have brought her hand into contact with a muscled thigh. It was totally unnerving, and she could not quite disguise the tremor in her hands.

'Do you take milk and sugar?' she enquired politely.

'Milk, but no sugar,' he replied, then the unexpected brush of his fingers against her own almost made her drop the tea cup as she handed it to him, and the gleam in his eyes made it embarrassingly clear that he was aware of her nervousness.

'How did that happen?' he asked at length, gesturing with a strong, well-shaped hand towards the cast on her leg.

'Against my better judgment I went horse-riding on a friend's farm, and the animal bucked me out of the saddle,' she explained, mentally recalling those terrifying moments when she had found herself so unexpectedly airborne. 'I broke my leg in two places.'

'When was this?'

'Three weeks ago.'

'I suppose this doesn't allow you much freedom to get about,' he concluded grimly.

'I manage on crutches,' Morgan smiled ruefully, 'but I was advised to stay off my leg to allow the bones to knit properly, and under no circumstances am I to put my weight on to that foot.'

Those incredibly blue eyes studied her thoughtfully, sliding over her lazily as if to acquaint themselves with her slender feminine curves until she felt her body become heated beneath the floral silk of her dress. He looked at her as if he was well aware of the mysteries of the female anatomy, and she felt oddly flushed and naked.

'I can't understand why we've never met before,' he said, his eyes lingering on her bright red-brown hair which tumbled in thick, lustrous waves down on to her slim, straight shoulders.

'Perhaps because I don't live and work here in Rossmere,' she managed in a tight, controlled voice.

'Where do you live?'

'Pretoria.'

His eyes flickered strangely. 'I go down to Pretoria quite often on business.'

'Do you?' she asked, attempting to sound un-interested, but Carl Ziegler was not to be put off.

'What kind of work do you do?' he continued his rapid inquisition.

'I'm private secretary to an attorney.'

'When do you expect your father home?'

He switched the topic of conversation so swiftly that, before she could prevent herself, she was saying, 'When my father plays golf it's an all-day game.'

'Wonderful!' Carl exclaimed, a satisfied gleam in his eyes.

'I beg your pardon?' she blinked, not quite sure what to make of him.

'What about coming for a drive with me?' he invited unexpectedly. 'It's a lovely day, we'll stop somewhere for lunch, and I'll have you home safe and sound this afternoon.'

Morgan shrank inwardly from the idea. 'Thank you for asking, but I——'

'Don't say no,' he interrupted hastily.

'I'm afraid I——'

'I couldn't bear to spend this beautiful day all on my own,' he cut into her refusal once again.

'I'm sure you must know plenty of women who would be only too willing to drop whatever they're doing to help fill the empty hours for you,' she argued mockingly.

'Oh, sure,' he gestured expressively towards the inside pocket of his jacket. 'I have my little black book handy for emergencies, but I'd much rather spend the day with you.' His hand was on her knee with a familiarity she had despised in others, and his smile was persuasive. 'Won't you say yes, Morgan . . . please?'

She stared at his hand, wanting to brush it away, but she had neither the strength nor the will to do so. The sensations spiralling up her thigh were positively electrifying, and at that moment she was willing to do almost anything to escape his touch.

'I shall have to change,' she croaked, unable to tear her eyes off that brown hand resting so naturally on her knee.

'You look fine just as you are,' he insisted, sliding his disturbing glance over her.

'If you wouldn't mind giving me a hand up, then I would like to go and pull a comb through my hair and leave a message for my father in case he arrives home before we do,' she tried again, and this time he released her knee to clasp her hands firmly.

Carl very gallantly helped her up on to her crutches, and his nearness was so disturbing that she felt a tremor of alarm pass through her. God help her if this man ever tried to make love to her, she thought, but the next instant she was admonishing herself severely for even thinking such thoughts.

'I'll be waiting right here, honey,' he smiled, trailing a playful finger along her cheek, and it was like fire against her flushed skin.

Morgan moved away from him and went into the house, her hands gripping the crutches so tightly that her knuckles showed white through the skin, and when she reached her bedroom she closed the door behind her almost as if she were afraid that he would follow her there.

This was ridiculous, she told herself, leaning against the door for a moment to catch her breath. She had been out with men before, so why should she let Carl Ziegler affect her in this alarming way? He was attractive, suave, and not at all like any of the men she had known before, but that, she told herself severely, was no reason to behave like a girl on her first encounter with the opposite sex. She was being over-cautious and over-sensitive because of what her father had told her about this man, she finally decided. If she could shut her mind to that, then she might be able to relax in his company.

When Morgan stepped out on to the terrace a few minutes later she saw that the door on the passenger side of the Porsche had been opened, and Carl was coming swiftly up the steps towards her.

'Lean on me, and put your crutches against the wall,' he ordered.

Guessing his intentions, she shied away from it mentally and said hastily, 'I'll manage, thank you.'

'Don't be such a stubborn young lady, and do as you're told,' he commanded, and for some reason she obeyed the authoritative note in his voice. With her left hand on his shoulder, and her weight firmly on her left leg, she placed her crutches against the wall beside the entrance of the house, and the next instant she was lifted high in his arms and carried down the steps towards his car. Necessity forced her to place her arms about his neck, but the feel of that hard male body against her own sent a quivering awareness sweeping along her nervous system. His arms were hard as steel about her waist and behind her knees, and he seemed to be carrying her as if she were no weight at all. When, at last, she was lowered carefully on to the front seat of the Porsche, he smiled down into her eyes. 'That was much quicker, and much easier, wouldn't you say?' he asked.

'Thank you,' Morgan murmured faintly, having difficulty in controlling the rampant beat of her heart.

'My pleasure, ma'am,' he saluted her comically.

'My crutches!' she reminded him anxiously when he was about to close the door.

'You won't be needing them while you're with me.'

'You can't possibly carry me around all over the place,' she protested with frantic visions of Carl perhaps having to carry her into the ladies' cloakroom somewhere.

'You have a point there.' His eyes laughed lazily down into hers as if he had read her thoughts, then he fetched her crutches and dropped them unceremoniously on to the back seat. 'We'll just leave them there and forget about them unless you need them.'

His hands were strong and capable on the wheel, she noticed some minutes later, and somehow she found herself relaxing in the luxurious interior of Carl's Porsche. He had driven several kilometres out of Rossmere in a northerly direction when he swung the car off the road and parked it beneath the overhanging branches of a tall acacia.

'Just smell that air,' he said, letting down his window and drawing the air audibly into his lungs, then he leaned back in his seat and smiled. 'It's good to be back in South Africa, and I've been telling myself that almost every day during the past months.'

Morgan eased herself back against the door to study him closely. His hair was so incredibly fair, and his skin so deeply tanned, that the contrast was striking. His eyes were heavy-lidded and deceptively lazy, but there was nothing lazy about that aura of suppressed energy that clung to him. His mind was alert, his jaw determined, but she suspected that many people were deceived by his outward appearance which gave the impression that he was a Don Juan, and no more than that.

'Do you still have family and business commitments in America?' she found herself questioning him.

'No family commitments, but business, yes,' he replied, resting his arm along the seat behind her shoulders. 'I couldn't simply discard what I was doing to come out here and take over my uncle's computer firm.'

'I suppose that requires a lot of travelling back and forth?'

'I'll say it does,' he admitted forcefully. 'But I'm hoping it won't be for much longer.'

'Does that mean you might return to the U.S.A. permanently, or do you intend to make your home here in South Africa?' she probed curiously.

'I haven't decided yet.' He waved an expressive hand, and turned in his seat to face her. 'Hey, gorgeous, I didn't bring you out on this lovely day to talk about myself.'

'What shall we talk about, then?' Morgan smiled unwillingly.

'*You* for a start.'

Her smile froze. 'I'm rather a dull subject.'

'I can't believe that.'

'It's the truth,' she insisted calmly. 'I've always led a terribly ordinary, dull life, and there's really nothing interesting or exciting about me.'

'That's a lie.' His blue glance slid over her with the sensual thoroughness of a professional. 'Right now I can think of several interesting and exciting things about you.'

'Your idea of interesting and exciting doesn't necessarily tally with mine,' she argued away the suggestion of intimacy in his deep voice.

'Doesn't it?' Her heightened colour did not escape him. 'I bet there've been plenty of men in your life.'

'Oh, yes, plenty,' she lied with a hint of mockery in her voice. 'So many that I've lost count of them.'

'Any of them serious?' he asked, studying her intently.

'Oh, all of them were serious.'

The brief silence was filled with birdsong and the shrill screeching of insects, then Carl said abruptly, 'You're not telling me the truth.'

'How clever of you to guess,' she smiled sarcastically as she capitulated. 'There has been no man in my life. No one special, that is,' she finally confessed.

'I guess what you're saying is that you've been out with a couple of guys, but none of them have ever taken your fancy.'

'You could say so, yes,' she nodded, growing tired of the topic of conversation.

'What do you look for in a man?' he probed relentlessly.

'I don't look for anything in particular, but I'll know when the right man comes along, and then . . .'

'I know,' he grunted almost as if he were in pain. 'Marriage, a home, and children.'

'What's wrong with wanting marriage, a home, and children?' she demanded defensively, eyeing him surreptitiously.

'Nothing, believe me,' he laughed cynically. 'It's just not my style, that's all.'

Morgan was not surprised, but she could not resist prodding him with, 'Is your freedom so important to you?'

'No one is ever free, my dear lady. We all have certain things that tie us, down, such as our obligations to those we work with, or work for, whichever the case may be, so there's really no such thing as total freedom in this life, but marriage is something quite different. Marriage is a total commitment of oneself, and I'm not the type to commit myself to one woman only for the rest of my life.' They sat there for a long time without speaking while the scent of the veld was all around them, then he glanced at her and smiled mockingly. 'You don't have anything to say to that?'

'What is there to say?' she shrugged her shoulders lightly 'We all live our lives in the way that suits us best, and it's not for me to condemn you for wanting to live your life free of the commitments involved in a marriage.'

'But you don't approve.'

She looked into those disturbing eyes, and away again quickly before he saw just how much their conversation was affecting her. 'Whether I approve or disapprove is inconsequential, Mr Ziegler. It's really none of my business.'

He reached out, and this time those strong brown

fingers gripped her right hand tightly. 'How many times do I have to tell you that my name is Carl?'

His touch had an odd effect on her vocal chords, and she had to take a deep, steadying breath before she said haltingly, 'Sorry . . . Carl.'

'That's better,' he smiled, and her heart did an uncomfortable somersault in her breast at the sight of it.

'Would you mind giving me back my hand?' she asked in a voice that was surprisingly calm considering the way her nerves were reacting to his touch, and his mocking laughter was soft on her ears as he released her hand and started the car.

CHAPTER TWO

CARL pulled in at an open-air restaurant about thirty kilometres from Rossmere, and without the slightest sign of embarrassment he lifted Morgan out of the car and carried her to a vacant table. She protested, but he paid no heed, and they ate their lunch beneath the dappled shade of a marula tree, but Morgan was more aware of her companion than of what she was eating.

'Morgan is an unusual name for a girl,' Carl remarked when they finally lingered over their coffee.

'It was my mother's surname before she married my father,' she explained with a grimace. 'I think they had hoped for a boy, but when I came along they must have decided that it would suit me just as well.'

'It does suit you,' he said, his glance sliding over her. 'It goes with your hair, your eyes . . .'

'I believe you said something about having no family ties,' she changed the subject hastily.

'I said I had no family commitments,' he corrected, looking amused. 'My mother died some years back, I have a sister back in the States, but my father and I have never seen eye to eye, and we sort of drifted apart, if you know what I mean.'

Morgan eyed him curiously. 'You don't see him often, then?'

'Not often,' he confessed cynically, 'and when we do meet the most we can manage is "Hi", "How are you", and "Goodbye".'

'That doesn't sound like a very healthy relationship to me,' she observed drily.

'The less we see of each other, the healthier it becomes,' he laughed derisively. 'Do you get on well with your father?'

'Very well,' she admitted thoughtfully. 'We have been even closer these past two years since my mother's death.'

'What did your father tell you about me?'

Momentarily caught off guard by his question, she very nearly blurted out the truth, but she took her time replying, and when she did there was a glimmer of amusement in her grey-green eyes. 'I don't think it would be good policy to discuss what my father said about the president and chairman of the company he works for, do you?'

'Now you've made me curious.' His narrowed eyes glittered with cynical humour. 'Come on, honey, you can tell me.'

'He said absolutely nothing to discredit you,' she prevaricated, shifting uncomfortably in her chair. 'In fact, he complimented you by saying that you were extremely clever with computers, and that you had an excellent head for business.'

'That's not all he said,' Carl prompted shrewdly.

'No, that's not all he said,' she replied with inherent honesty.

'Are you going to tell me the rest?'

'I thought women were supposed to be the nosey ones,' she laughed nervously.

'Tell me, Morgan.' The laughter had left his eyes. 'Tell me what he said that changed you from the friendly girl I met yesterday, into the reserved young woman I encountered this morning?'

Morgan hesitated. Would he understand her father's concern, or would he take exception to it? If she had been better acquainted with Carl Ziegler then she might have known what to say, but unfortunately she knew so very little about this man seated opposite her. She sensed an inner thread of steel behind that pleasant exterior, and something else she could not define. Could it be anger? She was a bad liar, she decided eventually, and Carl did not look the type of man who would accept half-truths from anyone.

'My father warned me to stay out of your way,' she said, watching the wild doves peck up the crumbs which the people were throwing to them. 'He said you had a reputation for changing your women more often than there were seasons in a year,' she concluded, repeating almost verbatim her father's words, and holding her breath for some reason.

'Is that a crime?' Carl asked, commanding her attention, and she met his cool glance with some trepidation.

'If no one has been hurt in the process, then I suppose not,' she ventured to give her opinion.

'Are you afraid of being hurt?'

'Aren't we all?'

He shrugged his broad shoulders nonchalantly. 'Some people more than others, perhaps, but I've always chosen my victims carefully, and then I've never promised anything I wasn't prepared to give.'

There was a sudden coolness in the air, or was it a coolness which came from within herself? 'You speak of victims, and not women.'

'If I have a big bad wolf image, then I imagine you

would consider the women I've known as victims of my lust.'

His mouth had tightened and his eyes had narrowed to slits of unfathomable blue fire. She wondered nervously what he was thinking, and before she could prevent herself she heard herself asking, 'Are you angry?'

'No, I'm not angry, but I'm downright curious,' he replied thoughtfully. 'I was wondering what made Little Red Riding Hood come out and play with the Big Bad Wolf.'

She did not need to be told that he was referring to her presence there with him, and the corners of her wide mouth lifted in an involuntary smile that conveyed the humorous side of her nature. 'My mother once told me that a man's behaviour towards a woman depended largely on the woman's behaviour towards the man.'

'In other words, a man shan't attempt to seduce a woman unless she has shown that she's willing to be seduced?' he questioned mockingly.

'Exactly.'

'I hate to say it, but your mother was right,' he said, leaning his elbows on the table, and studying her with a look in his eyes that sent the blood tripping a little faster through her veins. 'Had you been any one of a dozen other girls we would have been at my place making love instead of sitting here innocently, sharing a meal in the beautiful outdoors.'

'Talking of food,' she changed the subject hastily, hoping he did not notice her heightened colour, 'we've had lunch ages ago, and I really do think it's time you took me home.'

His strong, sensuous mouth curved in a mocking smile, then he settled the bill and lifted her out of her chair to carry her back to his car.

'My place or yours?' he asked finally with an element of seduction and mockery in his deep voice when he slid behind the wheel and leaned towards her.

'Mine,' she stated firmly. 'My father should be home any time now.'

'Ah, well, it was a lovely, fleeting hope, but——' He smiled at her with disarming confidence. 'Another time perhaps.'

Morgan's colour deepened, but she said nothing, and they drove back to Rossmere in silence. Carl Ziegler was truly the most extraordinary man she had ever met. He made no secret of what he wanted, and she would have had to be blind and senseless not to realise why he had so much success with women, but she was determined not to be added to his long list of conquests. If she ever decided to give herself to a man, then it would have to be for no other reason but love, and she doubted if Carl Ziegler would ever know the meaning of the word.

When they arrived at her home he lifted her in his arms for the fourth time that day and carried her up on to the terrace. Morgan sat rigidly on a cane chair which he had lowered her into, and her body still tingled after coming into contact with his as she watched him while he fetched her crutches from the car and placed them close at hand for her.

'I'll call you,' he said abruptly, taking her hand and raising it to his lips, and moments later his Porsche was speeding down the drive.

Morgan felt more than a little bemused as she sat there staring blindly after him. For some unaccountable reason the touch of his lips against her fingers had seemed to brand her for life, and she wondered crazily what it would feel like to have those very male lips pressed passionately against her own.

Angry with herself for thinking such absurd thoughts, she levered herself up on to her crutches, but before she could enter the house she saw her father's Mercedes coming up the drive, and she decided to wait for him instead.

'Was that Carl Ziegler I passed on the way?' Andrew wanted to know when he finally joined her on the terrace.

'Yes, Daddy.'

Andrew's eyes narrowed angrily. 'What did he want?'

'He came to see me,' she replied truthfully. 'He arrived here just before tea this morning, and invited me out to lunch.'

'And you went with him?'

'I did refuse at first, but——'

'He persuaded you,' her father filled in for her shrewdly, and she laughed softly and a little cynically.

'Oh, he's very persuasive.'

'And?' her father demanded anxiously.

'And nothing,' she said, moving awkwardly on the crutches as she preceded her father into the house. 'We went for a long drive into the country, we stopped at an open-air restaurant for lunch, and we talked.'

'Morgan . . .'

'I know,' she interrupted, pausing to gaze seriously up at her still handsome father. 'Don't get involved, you said, and I shan't, but I did enjoy his company, and it did help to pass the day.'

'Are you going to see him again?'

'He said he would call me, but I somehow doubt if he will,' she smiled a little ruefully. 'I'm not really his type, you see, and neither is he mine.'

As Morgan had predicted, she did not hear from Carl during the next few days. She deliberately avoided discussing him with her father, and neither did her father mention his name. Carl Ziegler had come in and out of her life so swiftly that she could almost convince herself that it had not happened, but he was not the kind of man one could dismiss entirely. He was too dynamic, too vital, and much too disturbingly male for any woman to ignore his existence, and, even though Morgan made an attempt to do so, she found him leaping into her thoughts at the oddest moments.

Almost two weeks had passed since that Sunday she had spent with Carl, and she was sunning herself out on the terrace one afternoon when Paulina's buxom figure came waddling towards her, her round black face wide-eyed and anxious.

'Telephone for you, Missy Morgan,' she said in her own peculiar brand of English. 'I tell the *baas* I take a message, but he say no, he speak only to Missy Morgan.'

'Did he give his name?' Morgan asked frowningly, reaching for her crutches, and getting awkwardly to her feet.

'No, Missy,' Paulina shook her turbaned head, 'but he talk funny. Not like our *baas*.'

Carl, the name leapt into Morgan's mind, but she dismissed the thought at once as ridiculous, and glanced reassuringly at the maid who stood hovering with uncertainty about her. 'Thank you, Paulina. I'll manage.'

Morgan entered the house as quickly as the crutches would allow her, and made her way through the living-room into the hall.

'Morgan Field speaking,' she said when she leaned against the wall and lifted the receiver to her ear.

'Hi there, sunshine.'

That deep, velvety, and unmistakably American voice almost made her drop the receiver, but she gripped it with renewed strength, and said calmly, 'Hello, Carl.'

'I'm sorry I took so long to call you, honey, but I've been in Washington on business, and I only got back late last night.'

'You don't owe me an explanation, Carl.'

'I wasn't explaining, I was stating a fact,' he answered abruptly, and there was a strained little silence before he asked softly, 'Did you miss me?'

She felt her heart hammering ridiculously against her ribs, and her breathing quickened as she asked, 'Should I have?'

'I missed you.'

'Don't be silly!' she laughed away his remark, but she could not laugh way that little thrill of pleasure that shot through her.

'When can I see you again?'

A mocking smile curved her mouth. 'I'm afraid I have a rather full schedule ahead of me. I'm going dancing this evening, and tomorrow I'm playing tennis at——'

'Morgan!' he interrupted sharply. 'Have dinner with me this evening?'

Her heart skipped a beat, but she said evasively, 'I shall have to consult my diary.'

'Morgan,' he groaned impatiently at the other end, 'I have a board meeting in two minutes flat. Give me a straight yes or no.'

Oh, God, she wanted to see him again, it was no use denying it and, against her better judgment, she heard herself say, 'Yes, Carl.'

'I'll call for you at seven,' he said, and the line went dead before she could retract her acceptance of his invitation.

Her hand was shaking visibly when she returned the receiver to its cradle, and despite all her efforts there was an unfamiliar excitement welling up inside of her. *Dinner with Carl.* What on earth had possessed her to say yes? Every instinct warned her to stay away from this man, yet the sound of his voice had been enough to dissolve all her firm resolutions into nothing. It was crazy, and totally illogical, but she was looking forward intensely to seeing him again.

'I'm having dinner with Carl this evening,' she informed her father when he arrived home late that afternoon. 'He's calling for me at seven.'

Andrew frowned fiercely. 'I don't like it, Morgan, and you know that.'

'I'll be careful,' she promised.

'You're going to get hurt.'

'Not if I can help it,' she insisted.

'I wish it was your arm that was broken, then you could always take a swing at his head if he tries any funny business.'

'Oh, Daddy,' she giggled uncontrollably, 'what terrible thoughts are milling through your head? Do you imagine he's going to cart me off to his love-nest with the intention of making passionate love to me on his settee?'

Andrew poured himself a stiff drink and swallowed down almost half of it before he said: 'If you don't know it yet, then you'll find out soon enough that that's his style exactly, or so I've been led to believe.'

'How enthralling!' she laughed mockingly.

'Don't joke about it, Morgan,' her father rebuked her with a troubled expression on his weary face.

'Sorry, Daddy,' she sobered instantly, but mischief still danced in her eyes. 'I could always kick him hard on the shins, I suppose.'

Andrew's mouth twitched, a sign that he appreciated her humour, but the frown remained, and Morgan could not exactly blame him for being concerned. If she had to be honest, then she was equally concerned about herself, but not for anything in the world was she going to let her father discover this. She would have dinner with Carl, there was no harm in that, but she knew that she would have to watch her step emotionally.

Morgan was in her room that evening when she heard Carl's Porsche come up the drive, and when she went into the living-room a few minutes later she found him indulging in a serious conversation with her father, but he turned at once at the sound of her crutches on the carpeted floor.

'Morgan, honey, it's good to see you,' he smiled, the devastating length and breadth of him in a dark evening suit blotting out her father's troubled face as he came towards her, and a devilish light leapt into his eyes as he spoke to her father without taking his glance away from Morgan's slim figure in the long-sleeved, full-length emerald green evening dress. 'You have a beautiful daughter, Andrew,' he said with obvious deliberation. 'She's quite the most beautiful girl I've seen in a long time, and I can't wait to get her to myself.'

'Carl!' Morgan hissed admonishingly so that only he could hear, then she glanced beyond him at her father. 'I shan't be home late, Daddy.'

'I've sure got your old man worried, haven't I?' Carl remarked mockingly when they were in the hall.

'You have,' Morgan admitted with a quiet rebuke in her faintly husky voice, 'and it wasn't very nice of you.'

'I couldn't help it,' Carl confessed. 'Honest, ma'am.'

'You're impossible!' she sighed, a hint of laughter in her eyes, but the laughter faded when he took her crutches from her and lifted her effortlessly into his arms. 'This really isn't necessary, you know,' she protested.

'If this is the only way I'll get to hold you in my arms, then I'll willingly carry you wherever you want to go,' he said, his breath fanning her cheek as he carried her out of the house to where he had parked his car. The moon turned his hair to pure silver, and the woody scent of his masculine cologne quivered in her nostrils. It stirred her senses, and turned an innocent situation into something dangerously intimate when he turned his head slightly to look at her. His arms tightened about her, and his eyes glittered strangely in the darkness as he murmured, 'I like your perfume. It reminds me of a sunny spring morning with the dew lying heavy on the grass. It's fresh, clean, and exciting.'

'Don't overdo it, Carl,' she warned hastily, conscious of his lips so close to her own, and that mad, surging desire to know their warmth against her own. 'I might just become suspicious and change my mind about having dinner with you.'

She felt him shaking with silent laughter. 'You're a tough nut, honey, but I'll crack you yet!'

'Where are we going?' she asked some minutes later when she realised that they were not driving in the direction of the town.

'To my place,' Carl announced, and a little shiver of shock made its unpleasant way through her. 'No comment?'

Morgan's fingers curled tightly about her evening purse. 'I can't say that I'm pleased about it, but I suppose I should have expected something like this.'

'There aren't many decent restaurants in Rossmere, and I have an excellent chef at home, so what better place to have dinner with you?'

'I'm not complaining . . . *yet*,' she said stiffly, casting a quick, nervous glance in his direction, and finding nothing reassuring in the brief smile he directed at her.

'That's my girl,' he murmured, and for one shattering moment his hand rested on her knee before he returned it to the steering wheel.

While Randolph Hillier enjoyed his retirement in his cottage along the Natal coast, Carl had come to consider his uncle's home his own. The sprawling, white-washed mansion stood on several acres against one of the sloping hills surrounding the town, and the interior was even more imposing than Morgan had imagined. It possessed a mixture of all the modern conveniences one could wish for, as well as expensive antiques which the Triton's founder had picked up on many of his travels across the world. Carl had made a few alterations in the living-room to suit his own personality, but basically it was still the same as before, Carl explained when he paused with her in his arms in the centre of the room.

'Do you like it?' he asked abruptly close to her ear.

Morgan stared at the zebra skin on the floor in front of the fireplace, the mounted kudu horns and ancient rifles against the wall above the mantelshelf, and felt a little stifled.

'It's all very masculine,' she admitted, adding reluctantly, 'It's nice, though.'

Those lazy blue eyes so close to hers mocking her suddenly. 'I knew you'd say that.'

That element of danger was there between them again, making her aware of the hard warmth of his arms, the solid wall of his chest against which she was resting, and a tingling sensation in the tips of her fingers as she knew a desire to stroke his sleek fair head. A smothered feeling settled in her chest, and an erratic little pulse was beating in her throat as she said with forced calmness, 'You can put me down now, I think.'

'Are you comfortable?' he queried when he had lowered her on to the sofa in front of the fire, and she was arranging the skirt of her long dress about her.

'Very . . . thank you.'

'Are you afraid to be here alone with me?' he questioned her mockingly while he poured a glass of wine for her, and something more lethal for himself.

'Do I have reason to be afraid?' Morgan asked when he handed her her glass and seated himself on the sofa beside her.

'I'm the big bad wolf, remember, and I devour little girls like you for breakfast every morning,' he reminded her with a leering grin.

'How terribly bad for the digestion!'

'You're unique,' he laughed, swallowing down a mouthful of whisky.

'Is that a polite way of telling me that I'm a freak?'

'I meant it as a compliment.' He loosened his tie and discarded his jacket, his movements accentuating the play of muscles beneath the white silk shirt, and the ice tinkled in his glass when he finally swallowed down another mouthful. 'I've never met anyone like you before, and I'm downright intrigued.'

A smile quivered on her lips. 'Have you never met a woman before who's capable of resisting you for more than half an hour?'

'That's the problem with most women.' There was a devilish gleam in his eyes. 'They spoil the chase by giving in too soon.'

'The hunter and the hunted,' she remarked drily, regaining her confidence.

'Does it excite you to know that I'm hunting you?'

'I don't feel as though I'm being hunted,' she lied calmly, and a little daringly, while her nerve-ends quivered at the very sight of a muscled thigh so close to her own. 'I've been here almost a half hour, totally at your mercy, and you haven't so much as touched me unnecessarily.'

'You're on the menu as an after-dinner delicacy,' Carl warned, and Morgan could not prevent the laughter which bubbled past her lips.

'Do I remind you of biscuits and cheese?'

'Hm . . .' he smiled, leaning towards her in a way that quickened her pulse alarmingly. 'As fragile as a biscuit, and as spicy as cheese. When I sink my teeth into you, your defences will crumble.'

'You scare me out of my wits,' she informed him, feigning fear.

'You're a liar, Morgan Field,' he announced, his eyes searching hers. 'I've made you aware of me, yes, but I don't scare you at all and, if I'm not mistaken, then you're actually laughing at me.'

He was clever, she thought. Much too clever to be fooled by her, or anyone else. 'Would it dent your ego if I admitted that I found you amusing rather than frightening?'

'It wouldn't dent my ego at all. In fact it would be a refreshing change to know that you don't take me seriously.' Their eyes met and held for breathtaking seconds. 'I'm not really the big bad wolf, you know.'

'I know,' she heard herself replying in a faintly sarcastic tone. 'You're merely a virile man in search of someone to satisfy your physical needs, and it doesn't really matter to you where or with whom you find it.'

Carl flinched dramatically, and howled like a wounded animal. 'I think I prefer the big bad wolf image to the latest tag you're wanting to pin on me!'

'The truth usually hurts, doesn't it?' she smiled faintly.

'Ouch!' he winced realistically.

'I hit the target every time, it seems,' she observed, studying him closely.

'You were a little offsides, Morgan honey,' he told her with an odd tightness about his mouth. 'I enjoy the company of beautiful women, what full-blooded male wouldn't, and if the relationship leads to something more, then I would be the last one to complain. I'm willing, if they're willing, and that about sums it up.'

She sipped at her wine to steady that peculiar little quiver racing through her insides. 'I hope you don't imagine I'll become a willing participant in these games you play?'

'This is no game, Morgan,' he warned with a look in his eyes she could not fathom. 'It's real, it's factual, and the reason I'm biding my time with you is because it isn't often that I meet an intelligent, quickwitted young lady who stimulates me mentally. . .' His eyes wandered over her, lingering appreciatively on the clearly defined curve of her breasts and hips, '. . . as well as physically,' he added.

Morgan felt her skin burning as if he had actually touched her intimately with one of those strong, capable-looking hands, but she pulled herself together sharply.

'You're a rogue, Carl,' she accused.

'But a nice rogue, wouldn't you say?'

A smile plucked at her lips. 'I haven't quite made up my mind about that.'

He leaned towards her, and she knew instinctively that he was going to kiss her, but the next instant a sound at the door made him glance over his shoulder,

and a white-coated servant appeared, to announce that
dinner was to be served. Morgan felt relieved, but Carl
appeared to be faintly irritated at what she had felt was
a timely intrusion.

Their meal was served to them on trays in front of
the living-room fire, eliminating the embarrassing
necessity of her having to be carried into the dining-
room. Carl's chef had prepared creamy mushroom
soup, the tiniest potatoes, garden fresh carrots and
peas, and the most delicious chicken pie Morgan had
ever tasted. They drank wine, and they talked a great
deal, and they finished off the meal with a fruit salad,
and the inevitable cheese and biscuits before their
coffee was served.

'What business commitments do you still have in
America?' she questioned him eventually when the
trays had been removed. 'Or shouldn't I be prying?'

'There's no reason why you shouldn't know.' He
stirred his coffee thoughtfully and stared at the fire as
if he were seeing many kilometres across the Atlantic
Ocean. 'I have a computer company in Washington,
D.C. that's doing exceptionally well, then I have a
small ranch out in Wyoming where I keep a few
hundred head of cattle.'

Morgan felt vaguely surprised at the latter. 'I presume you have someone taking care of all this for you
while you're here in South Africa?'

'I have, naturally.'

He must have felt her studying him intently, for their
eyes met suddenly, and she plunged blushingly into an
explanation. 'You have the image of the successful
businessman stamped all over you, and I can't somehow imagine you on a cattle ranch.'

He smiled lazily. 'Can't you?'

'You're too polished for that kind of life,' she argued.

'I'd like to take you out there some time just to show you how wrong you are.'

Morgan felt it safer not to comment on that remark. She would have loved to travel to America to see his ranch, but most certainly not under the circumstances he envisaged.

'More wine?' he offered, removing her empty cup when she had finished her coffee.

'No, thank you.'

'Come on, just a little.'

'Are you trying to make me tipsy?' she demanded suspiciously, placing her hand over her glass to prevent him from filling it.

Carl grinned wickedly. 'The thought did cross my mind.'

'That doesn't surprise me at all,' she declared, wondering whether she should kick him in the shins *now*, or later. 'With my head spinning I'd be easier to seduce, wouldn't I?'

'Relax, Morgan,' he laughed easily, sliding his arm along the back of the sofa, and running his fingers lightly through her hair. 'Haven't I behaved myself impeccably all evening?'

'You have,' she admitted at once, trying to ignore the tingling sensation racing across her scalp with his fingers brushed against the nape of her neck.

'Then what are you worried about?'

'I'm simply trying to decide when you're most likely to pounce,' she confessed bluntly. 'I'd like to be prepared for it, you see.'

'I never pounce,' he assured her, his voice vibrantly low and seductive. 'I prefer to take it nice and easy. It's much more enjoyable that way.'

There was something so boldly sexual in his statement that every instinct within her warned her to steer clear. 'I think we should change the subject.'

'Do you?'

He leaned towards her, his fingers like fire against her skin as he raised her face to his, and something in the way his eyes lingered on her mouth made her realise the danger she was drifting into.

'Carl!' she warned sharply and, almost as if he anticipated her physical withdrawal, he slid his hand beneath her hair until it rested against the nape of her neck.

'You're beautiful with the firelight dancing in your eyes.'

'Don't be ridiculous,' she rebuked him, hiding her panic behind a shield of mockery.

'Do you know something?' he said, the sheer maleness of him setting her pulses racing wildly. 'We've been talking too much.'

She knew she should have pulled away from him, but something more than just the light touch of his hand at the base of her skull held her immobile. His face became a blur, and her eyelids fluttered down a fraction of a second before his lips brushed against hers. His kisses were exploratory, testing and tasting almost as if he were savouring her lips and trying to decide whether he liked it or not. They were passionless kisses, but deep down inside Morgan something quivered to life; something which she found difficult to suppress, and which she found vaguely disturbing when she recognised it as an aching longing. She was kissing him back without actually intending to, and a thousand little nerves came alive beneath his fingers as they trailed caressingly along her throat.

She raised a hand to push him away, but her fingers somehow slipped between his shirt buttons to come into contact with warm, hair-roughened flesh. She heard the sharp intake of his breath, and the next instant his arms were like steel bands about her, crushing her softness against the hard wall of his chest so that she could feel his heart beating hard and fast in unison with hers. She tried to struggle free, but there was no escape, and the hard, sensual warmth of his mouth drove her lips apart. She tried not to respond, but his intimate invasion of her mouth sent her spinning into a vortex of emotions that made her mind reel crazily. She had been kissed before, but never like this, and never had she been more reluctant to leave a man's arms than she was at this moment to leave Carl's.

CHAPTER THREE

TIME seemed to stand still for Morgan. She was conscious only of Carl's mouth against her own, his hands moving urgently against her back, and her own clamouring response. It would be so easy to lose herself in his embrace, but she had to remember that this was purely a game to Carl, a brief encounter which he would soon forget. Her surrender would mean no more to him than that of any other woman he had known in the past, while to her . . .! She halted her alarming thoughts abruptly, and stirred against him.

'Was that so bad?' he asked, his eyes quizzical as he drew a little away from her.

Morgan pulled herself together with an effort, and shifted further out of his embrace. 'I could think of worse things that have happened to me.'

'Shall we try it again?'

'No!' Her hands were flat against his chest, holding him off when he would have drawn her closer. 'I think it's time you took me home.'

'But it's still so early,' he mocked her.

'It's almost eleven,' she argued, her voice surprisingly even as she glanced at the clock on the mantelshelf, 'and I know my father won't sleep a wink tonight until he knows I'm safe and sound at home.'

Carl released her slowly, but his mocking eyes never left her face. 'You think he's sitting at home biting his fingernails to the bone and wondering whether I've succeeded in luring you into bed with me?'

'I'm sure he is, and I think he has every right to be concerned,' she replied coolly, taking into consideration how she had reacted to his kisses.

'My reputation must be pretty bad,' he observed drily.

'It's not your reputation that bothers my father, it's my inexperience with men like yourself that troubles him most,' she retorted honestly.

'He thinks of you as his innocent little girl?' Carl laughed shortly, a measure of disbelief in his expression.

'He doesn't *think* it, he *knows* it.'

Carl's fingers were beneath her chin, forcing her to meet his eyes. 'You mean no man has ever made love to you?'

'Does that surprise you?'

'It pleases me more than anything else,' he said, his mouth curving sensually. 'It means that I'll be the first.'

'Not if I can help it,' she retorted sharply, brushing his hand away. 'I'm old-fashioned in that respect. I believe in marriage with all the responsibilities and commitments attached to it, and sex will simply have to wait until then.'

His hand lifted a thick wave of hair away from her flushed face, and his eyes had a near-hypnotic effect on her as he murmured thickly, 'I'll have to see what I can do about changing your mind on that score.'

'Take me home, Carl,' she whispered unsteadily, knowing that if she prolonged this moment she would have no will left to resist him. 'Please, Carl?'

His eyes mocked her as if he was totally aware of the struggle going on inside of her, then he smiled faintly. 'How can I refuse when you ask so nicely?'

He put on his jacket, then he picked her up in his arms and carried her out of the warm house into the cold, star-studded night. There was no way she could avoid this physical contact, and even though those hard arms held her impersonally, her thudding heart seemed unaware of the difference.

Carl drove her home in silence, and neither did Morgan attempt to make conversation. It was, after all, a pleasant silence between them, without any turbulent undercurrent of emotions, and it gave her time to think. Where was this association with Carl leading to? Perhaps it would have been more to the point to ask herself where *she* wanted it to lead to. That shook Morgan considerably. Where *did* she want it to lead to? A lighthearted affair with no commitments on either side? She shook her head adamantly in the dark interior of the car, grateful that Carl could not see her properly while he concentrated on his driving, and a few minutes later he was parking the Porsche in the driveway of her home.

He carried her into the house without speaking, but instead of relinquishing his burden when they entered the dimly-lit hall, she felt his arms tighten about her.

'You can put me down now, Carl,' she said quickly, looking into those very blue eyes and seeing them darken with something close to desire. 'My crutches are there against the wall, and I'll manage,' she tried to distract him.

He lowered her until her feet almost touched the floor, but, instead of releasing her, his arm tightened about her waist, and his lips descended towards hers. She tried to turn her head away to avoid his kiss, but his hand was in her hair, holding her head still, and despite her valiant efforts her lips quivered responsively beneath his as he held her suspended against the hard length of his body. His mouth was warm and sensual, arousing her with a practised ease until it felt as if her head was spinning with the rush of blood pounding through her veins. An eternity seemed to pass before he raised his head, and her heart was beating so hard and fast that it took her a while to find her voice.

'Thank you for an enjoyable evening,' she said, trembling from head to foot, and looking everywhere but into those mocking blue eyes as he handed her the crutches.

'Goodnight, Morgan honey,' the deep velvet of his voice caressed her and, taking her face between his hands, he kissed her lightly on the lips once more. 'Dream of me, will you?'

Morgan was still standing there in the hall with a bemused expression on her face when Carl drove away from her father's home. The feel and taste of his lips was still on hers, and she was not yet ready to confront her father when she heard his firm step behind her.

'Are you going to spend the rest of the night in the hall?' he demanded curiously, and the colour in her cheeks deepened with annoyance and embarrassment.

'No, of course not,' she said abruptly, the rubbers on the crutches thumping almost agitatedly on the floor as she moved.

'Morgan . . .'

She knew instinctively what was on her father's mind and, glancing at him over her shoulder, she said reassuringly, 'Nothing happened, Daddy.'

'I'm not so sure of that.'

Her eyes widened. 'What do you mean?'

'Don't fall in love with him, Morgan.'

His quietly spoken warning triggered off her sense of humour, but her laughter was stifled in her throat before a sound had passed her lips.

'Goodnight, Daddy,' her own voice reached her ears as if from a distance, and a few minutes later she was alone in her bedroom without actually being aware of how she had got there.

She pulled herself together with some difficulty. This was the third time she had seen Carl Ziegler in a matter of two weeks, and she was not going to allow herself to think anything beyond the fact that she had enjoyed his company. Within the next week she would be returning to Pretoria, and after that she did not imagine that she would see him again. Carl was not the type of man to waste his time with one woman while there were so many others who were only too willing to fall into bed with him at the snap of his fingers. It would not matter to her at all if she never saw him again, and she would forget him as easily as she had forgotten all the other men who had wandered in and out of her life.

Morgan felt cold and miserable when she got into bed that night, and the cast on her leg felt heavier than ever before. She tried not to think of Carl, but he was there in her mind as if he intended to stay. He was not someone she would forget in a hurry, she admitted with some reluctance. He was too vital, and too supremely

masculine, for any woman to forget him the moment
he was out of their sight. Besides that the memory of
his kisses was still too hauntingly fresh, and without
any considerable effort she could still feel those strong
arms holding her. His mere physical presence had
made her aware of her femininity in a way no other
man had done before, and his kisses had aroused emotions which she had not known she possessed. It had
not frightened her at the time, but it frightened her
now. Oh, he was very clever where women were concerned, and she had no doubt that his experience had
taught him a great deal—too much, perhaps, for the
comfort of someone like herself.

'Dream of me,' Carl had said before he had left her
that evening, and that was exactly what Morgan did.
Her dreams revolved around him, then with one
woman, and then with another clinging to his arm, and
inviting his kiss. Morgan saw it all as if she were
standing outside a shop window looking in, but he
never looked her way, not even to acknowledge her
existence, and it hurt . . .oh, *how* it hurt! When she
eventually awoke from this dream there were tears on
her cheeks, and a terrible tightness in her chest. If he
could do this to her in her dreams, then how much
more could he do to hurt her in reality, and it was then
that she decided not to see him again.

There was no difficulty in avoiding Carl during the
remainder of her stay in Rossmere. He telephoned her
on the Thursday evening to tell her that he was flying
down to Cape Town on business the following morning, and he did not expect to be back before the
Wednesday evening of the week thereafter. That suited

Morgan perfectly. She would be leaving Rossmere the morning immediately after Carl's return. She would write him a brief, friendly note thanking him for his kindness, and that would be that.

It did not work out quite as Morgan had hoped it would. She was packing her suitcases the Wednesday afternoon when Paulina told her that she had a visitor waiting to see her in the living-room, and her heart almost leapt out of her breast a few minutes later when she saw the tall, fair-haired man at the window turn away from his contemplation of the garden to face her.

'Carl!' she croaked nervously. 'I thought you said you'd be back this evening?'

'I concluded my business a day sooner than I'd expected.' For the first time since knowing him his hooded eyes were cold and angry as he lessened the distance between them with a few lithe strides. 'Why didn't you tell me you were returning to Pretoria tomorrow?'

Morgan's calm expression belied the utter chaos of her emotions at that moment as she found herself looking a long way up into his face. 'I didn't think it would interest you.'

'Dammit, of course I'm interested!' he barked furiously.

'Why?' she smiled, resorting to sarcasm. 'Because you still haven't succeeded in getting me into bed with you?'

His jaw hardened, and his nostrils flared with anger. 'That's one of the reasons.'

'Please do tell me the others?'

'I'll tell you when I'm good and ready for it.'

'Why don't you admit that it's the only reason?' she

chided him relentlessly, and a dangerous light entered his heavy-lidded eyes.

'Why don't we quit this ridiculous argument?' he ground out the words, and the next instant his arms were locked about her waist.

The grip on her crutches broken, they fell with a thud on to the carpeted floor, but she was only barely conscious of it when his mouth swooped down to claim hers with a passionate anger that left her shaken to her very foundations, and her heart was pounding so wildly against her ribs that she could hardly breathe when he slipped an arm behind her knees and carried her towards the sofa.

'Oh, Carl, this is all really too absurd,' she protested weakly when she found herself lying down against the cushions while he leaned over her with a menacing gleam in his incredibly blue eyes.

'Why didn't you tell me?' he demanded bluntly, his hands against her shoulders forcing her to remain where she was when she tried to get up.

'I was going to leave a note for you,' she defended herself.

'You were, were you?' he remarked scathingly. 'And I suppose it would have been an impersonal little note saying, "It was nice knowing you, and goodbye"?'

An involuntary smile plucked at the corners of her mobile mouth. 'It wouldn't have been quite so abrupt.'

'Oh, yeah?'

'Yeah,' she mimicked him daringly.

'Your accent's lousy,' he accused in a less aggressive manner.

'So is yours,' she hit back. 'You don't even speak the Queen's English.'

'Witch,' he grinned. 'How dare you criticise me!'

'I dare because you're behaving like a positive beast, and——'

His mouth covered hers, sealing off the rest of her tirade, and her lips parted almost as if she had invited his intimate invasion of her mouth, and the erotic sensations it aroused. His male warmth seemed to envelope her, and she welcomed it until his hands moved from their exploration of her slim shoulders down to her breasts. Through the thin cotton of her blouse her body responded diabolically to the caress of his fingers, and she stirred protestingly beneath him, forcing her hands between them until she managed to thrust him from her.

'Stop it, Carl, and let me go,' she insisted, her voice a little huskier than usual, and her cheeks flushed. 'I have a lot of packing to do before I leave here tomorrow morning, and my father wants to leave early.'

'Your daddy's not taking you,' Carl announced calmly, brushing a strand of hair away from her cheek and twisting it playfully about his finger. 'I am.'

'Oh, no!'

'Oh, *yes*!' he laughed softly down into her surprised face. 'It's all arranged, and I'll be here at eight in the morning to pick up.'

'But I——' A wave of helplessness swept over her, and her hands fluttered in an expressive gesture against his chest. 'I give up.'

A wicked look leapt into his eyes. 'Does that mean——'

'No, it doesn't,' she interrupted hastily, her colour deepening and her pulse quickening at the sexual undercurrent in the conversation.

'Pity,' he murmured mockingly, his glance on the agitated rise and fall of her small breasts.

'I'm not going to hop into bed with you, Carl,' she insisted quietly and adamantly even while every nerve quivered in response to his nearness. 'Not today, not tomorrow, not *ever*,' she added firmly.

'I wouldn't bet on that, honey,' he smiled, his fingers sliding in a sensual caress across her cheek to seek out that sensitive hollow beneath her ear, and she could not suppress those deliciously primitive sensations that shivered through her.

'Don't you ever give up?' she croaked.

'Not when I have a hunch that I'm on to something good,' he stated blandly, and he had the look of a Viking who knew he was more than halfway to victory.

His confidence in himself frightened her. It frightened her even more when she thought of how vulnerable she had become. He attracted her physically in a way she had never thought possible, and even now those caressing fingers against her cheek and throat were kindling fires that filled her with a deep-seated longing she had never known before. Her father had been right all along. She should have taken a firmer stand that very first time Carl had invited her to have lunch with him, but he had been so incredibly persuasive, and she had been so damnably easy to persuade, she recalled agitatedly.

'Would you mind handing me my crutches, and allowing me to get up?' she broke the silence between them, a coolness in her voice which he could not avoid hearing.

Those caressing fingers stilled against her throat, and a few moments later she was standing upright, and leaning heavily on her crutches while she tried to avoid the probing intensity of his eyes.

'Why do I get the feeling that you're annoyed about something?' he demanded, sensing the change in her mood accurately.

'I can't possibly allow you to take me to Pretoria tomorrow,' she announced on an unmistakable note of protest. 'I have to see the specialist to have this cast removed, I'll have to be X-rayed, and quite likely another cast will have to be put on. It might take all day.'

'I will have the entire day to take you wherever you want to go.'

'But, Carl, I——' Morgan's eyes traced the unrelenting line of his jaw, and she knew without being told that she was fighting a losing battle. 'Oh, what's the use!' she sighed irritably.

'You don't want me to take you, is that it?'

She looked up into those heavy-lidded yes, and felt compelled to say, 'To be quite honest with you, Carl, I think our association should end right here and now.'

'Why?' he shot out the question.

'Because you're wasting your time,' she answered tritely, aware of the tension between them which she had placed there. 'I don't want to find myself caught up in a senseless affair with you.'

Her words hovered like an accusation in the air between them, and his tight-lipped expression sent a sudden chill up her spine.

'Would you settle for friendship?'

'Oh, Carl!' she laughed helplessly at his unexpected query, and her laughter seemed to fan his anger.

'What's so funny about wanting to be friends?' he

demanded harshly, and she sobered at once only to find that she was horrifyingly close to tears.

'Your persistence is flattering,' she said, controlling herself admirably, 'but we can never be friends ... and you know that.'

His eyes narrowed perceptibly. 'Be ready at eight sharp tomorrow morning.'

It was only when she heard his car go down the drive that Morgan realised she was shaking all over as if she had caught a chill. She had angered him, she knew that, and quite suddenly she felt sick inside.

She felt heavy-hearted when she continued her packing that afternoon, and it was not until she had had dinner with her father that evening that she had the opportunity to speak to him about Carl.

'Did you tell Carl I'd be returning to Pretoria tomorrow?' she questioned Andrew, and an angry frown creased his brow.

'He must have found out somehow that I wouldn't be coming in to the office tomorrow, and questioned me about it.'

'How could you have agreed to let him take me?'

'I put up an argument, but he was insistent,' Andrew admitted reluctantly. 'I'm sorry, Morgan. You know I would have done anything to avoid this, but Carl wouldn't take no for an answer, and I couldn't very well tell him to go to the devil.'

'I'm well acquainted with his persistent attitude,' she sighed resignedly. 'Oh, well, I shall just have to make the best of it, shan't I?'

Andrew had nothing to say to that except to shrug his shoulders with a helplessness which she felt equally acutely at that moment as if a weight had invaded her limbs. She felt trapped, and it was a feeling that persisted until she finally managed to fall asleep that night.

Carl arrived punctually at eight the following morning, and even at a glance she could see that his mood had not changed from that of the day before. His curiously detached attitude disturbed her intensely, and their conversation was brief and stilted while he deposited her suitcases in the boot of his car and helped her into the passenger seat.

They travelled for almost twenty kilometres without speaking a word, and Morgan began to sense that he was waiting for her to make the first move. Resentment stirred within her, but she finally relented when she could bear the silence between them no longer.

'If I sounded terribly ungracious yesterday, then I apologise, and it's really terribly kind of you to have offered to take me to Pretoria this morning,' she managed somehow.

'My reasons for wanting to take you had nothing to do with kindness, honey.'

Her nerves jarred uncomfortably. 'What were your reasons, then, if it was not out of kindness?'

'It's an opportunity to spend some time with you, and also to see where you live.'

Morgan folded her trembling hands tightly in her lap and, taking a careful breath, she asked warily, 'You have intentions of visiting me in future?'

'Would you object?' he counter-questioned, his eyes mocking as he glanced at her briefly.

'I doubt whether it would make any difference to you how I felt about it,' she accused with an inward sigh of resignation, and once again they lapsed into an awkward silence.

She stared straight ahead of her at the ribbon of road that wound its way through the sun-drenched, picturesque countryside, but she was unaware of anything except that sinking feeling at the pit of her stomach for which she could find no explanation.

'What time is your appointment with the specialist?' Carl asked suddenly, and she almost jumped nervously at the sound of his deep voice above the hum of the engine.

'Ten-thirty,' she answered him. 'There's time to unload my suitcases at the flat, and we could have a quick cup of coffee before we call on the specialist at the hospital.'

'That sounds great,' he smiled, and her heart lifted fractionally at the sight of it.

Less than an hour later Carl's Porsche slid to a halt outside a block of flats close to the city centre in Pretoria, and when he walked round the bonnet to her side with the intention of carrying her into the building, Morgan drew back sharply.

'My crutches, Carl.'

'You're being stubborn,' he accused.

'Please, Carl, I insist.'

Their glances clashed, and this time Morgan won. He took the crutches off the back seat and handed them to her, then he walked round to the boot and hauled out her suitcases.

They took the lift up to the seventh floor and, when they paused outside her door, she turned to him and said almost apologetically, 'Don't expect too much, will you? I rent a furnished flat.'

Without a word Carl took the key out of her hands

and inserted it in the latch, then he pushed open the panelled door, and stood aside for her to enter. The flat had been cleaned and aired regularly during her absence, and the polished pine furniture, with its bright floral cushions, was a welcome sight after her long sojourn in the country.

'Not bad,' Carl remarked, glancing about him appreciatively, then he gestured towards the suitcases in his hands. 'Where do I put these?'

'In the bedroom,' she said, pointing towards the short passage which led off the lounge. 'Through there.'

While he deposited her suitcases in the bedroom, Morgan went into the small kitchen, but she was still struggling to tap water into the electric kettle when Carl walked in, and his large frame seemed to dwarf the room considerably.

'If you tell me where everything is, I'll make the coffee,' he offered, and she did not put up an argument when he took the kettle from her and filled it with water.

Seated on a high stool beside the counter which served as a table, she told him where the cups, the sugar and the coffee were kept, then she left him to it.

'What about milk?' Carl asked at length.

'There should be some in the refrigerator,' she told him. 'When I telephoned yesterday the caretaker offered to get whatever supplies I might need.'

'Male or female?'

'I beg your pardon?' she blinked at him in blank confusion.

'The caretaker,' he explained his query. 'Male or female?'

'Oh!' She coloured slightly and smiled. 'Male, married and elderly.'

'That's a relief,' he grinned.

Their eyes met across the short distance separating them, and she laughed for no other reason than to relieve the tension between them. 'You sound like a jealous husband.'

'Heaven forbid!' he grimaced. 'I'll never be a husband, jealous or otherwise, but I am very possessive about my women.'

'I'm not one of your women, Carl,' she protested distastefully.

He did not comment on her statement as he placed her cup of coffee on the counter at her elbow, and joined her there on the spare stool. He raised his cup and smiled at her across the rim. 'Cheers.'

'*Gesondheid*,' she responded, raising her own cup to her lips.

It was a strange experience to be sitting there with Carl in her cramped kitchen. She was not in the habit of entertaining men in her flat, and his male presence in her strictly feminine domain filled her with an uneasiness she could not explain. His knee brushed accidentally against hers when he shifted his position, and she almost spilled the remainder of her coffee when sparks of awareness shot up her leg.

'Excuse me,' she said abruptly, putting down her cup and arranging her crutches so that she could ease her weight on to them. 'We haven't much time left, and I'd better get myself ready.'

She felt his eyes following her as she escaped laboriously into the bathroom, and when she encountered her image in the mirror above the basin she could not help thinking she looked like a very scared rabbit. Her grey-green eyes looked enormous, and her full, sensitive mouth had a tightness about it that suggested an inner tension.

'Pull yourself together,' she told herself severely. 'Carl Ziegler is a man, not a monster.'

Her image in the mirror seemed to mock her. 'It's not Carl Ziegler you're afraid of, is it? It's your own reaction to him that frightens you.'

She passed a tired, shaky hand over her eyes. It was crazy to feel this way, but right from the start he had awakened the most primitive emotions within her, and *yes*, it frightened her to think that one man had such a disturbing ability to shatter her well-adjusted life.

She fought a silent battle with herself while she freshened herself up, and she was relatively calm when she joined Carl a few minutes later, but he must have sensed some of the turmoil in her soul as he came towards her and framed her face in his strong, sensitive hands.

'I never want to hurt you, Morgan,' he said, his voice like soft velvet caressing and soothing her quivering nerves. 'You must believe that, honey.'

She tried to speak, but her throat felt too tight, and then the opportunity was lost when his mouth covered hers with an unexpected tenderness which was almost her undoing. The desire to lean against him, to feel the rock-hard support of his body against her own, was so intense that she had to rely upon every vestige of strength she possessed not to give in, and she was trembling with the effort when he finally eased his lips from hers.

'We'd better go, or you'll be late,' he said, his eyes lingering on her soft, quivering mouth, then he released her abruptly and walked away from her to open the door.

The rest of the day passed swiftly and without

further emotional incidents, but that did not mean it was a day without traumas of a different nature. Morgan's leg was X-rayed after the cast had been removed and, as she had feared, her leg was once again encased in a plaster cast which she would have to wear for yet another three weeks, but this time they put a metal, rubber-wedged object into the heel which would at least allow her to walk about without the aid of those infernal crutches. It was an all-day business, as Morgan had warned Carl, and there had been time for no more than a quick lunch at a restaurant not far from the hospital.

It was after four o'clock that afternoon when they finally returned to her flat, and it was there that Carl, who had been a tremendous help all day, asked curiously, 'What happens next?'

'I shall be returning to work tomorrow,' she told him firmly when they sat in the lounge sipping a much-needed cup of coffee. 'I've been away long enough, and I'm at least more mobile than I was before.'

'What will you do for transport?'

'I have a small Mini, but I'll make use of our excellent bus service until this cast is removed.'

'I don't fancy the idea of leaving you here alone.'

'Good heavens, Carl!' she laughed incredulously. 'I shall be perfectly all right.'

'I don't know when I'll be able to see you again,' he said at length, placing his cup on the tray and getting to his feet to pace the floor as if he were agitated about something. 'I'm going to be rather tied up during the next few weeks.'

She stared at the back of his fair head and the width of his shoulders in the brown suede jacket, and tried desperately not to read something into that statement which was not there. 'I know how busy you are, and I want you to know that I do appreciate the fact that you placed yourself at my disposal for the entire day.'

'That isn't what I meant, and you know it!' He was beside her on the sofa in an instant, and he gripped her hands so tightly that she almost cried out with the agony of it. 'You could at least tell me you'll miss me, and that you'll be thinking of me while I'm away,' he prompted, his eyes seeking hers.

'I'll miss you, and I'll be thinking of you,' Morgan felt compelled to say.

'You don't sound as if you mean it.'

'Oh, Carl!' she croaked, hovering somewhere between the desire to laugh and cry. 'Must you make everything so complicated?'

'Am I expecting too much?'

'You spoke of friendship yesterday,' she began, forcing herself to meet those deceptively lazy eyes. 'Let that be enough for now?'

'I accept that,' he nodded, pressing her hands against his chest where she could feel the hard warmth of his body through his expensive silk shirt. 'You will miss me, won't you?'

'Yes,' she heard herself whispering with more conviction this time, 'I'll miss you.'

Morgan was never certain afterwards whether she had moved towards him, or he towards her, but suddenly she was in his arms with her head buried against the hollow of his wide shoulder while his mouth devoured hers with devastating effects. When, at last, he released her and got to his feet, she felt peculiarly drained and lightheaded.

'Any messages for your father?'

It took a few moments for his words to sink in sufficiently for her to grasp his query, then she shook her head abruptly. 'I'll telephone him this evening.'

There was a hint of mockery in his smile as he leaned over her and brushed his lips lightly against hers. 'I'll be seeing you, honey.'

He was gone before she could think of anything to say which would detain him. Did she actually want to persuade him to stay longer? No, of course she didn't, but his vital presence still lingered in the room, and her lips still tingled with the memory of his fierce kisses. *I'll be seeing you*, he had said, and even while her mind rejected the thought, her treacherous heart was whispering, 'Make it soon!'

CHAPTER FOUR

MORGAN was back at her desk the following morning at the offices of Kelly, Eaton & De Vos, Attorneys at Law, and when Richard Kelly breezed in shortly after nine that morning, his rugged features creased into a welcoming smile at the sight of her. Only a few inches taller than Morgan, and stockily built, he paused beside her desk.

'It's good to have you back, Morgan,' he announced in his gravelly voice as he gripped her hand briefly.

'It's good to *be* back, Mr Kelly,' she replied with an eagerness and sincerity her employer would not have understood unless he had lived through weeks of idleness which had been concluded in an emotional turmoil.

He glanced down at the new cast on her leg. 'You're not out of the woods yet, I notice.'

'Three more weeks, that's all.'

'I hope you think twice in future before you accept another invitation to go riding,' he observed with a certain severity.

'I never was very good with horses,' she laughed lightly, 'and now, I think, I've lost my nerve completely.'

'I'm relieved to hear it,' he sighed, turning towards the communicating door. 'When you're ready, I have a few letters to dictate.'

Richard Kelly was a strange man, Morgan decided

while she sharpened her pencil and searched for her notebook. He was always reasonably friendly, but also strangely aloof, and after working for him for three years she still had no idea what went on inside that clever head of his when he was not working on a case. He was a bachelor, and he lived alone in a rambling old house on the outskirts of Pretoria, but he kept his private life *very* private, and Morgan had never pried, even though at times she had been curious.

She tapped briefly on his door a few moments later, and limped inside. His grey eyes smiled at her across the wide expanse of his desk when she had seated herself, he enquired politely whether she was comfortable, and then he started dictating in earnest.

During the course of the next two weeks it seemed to Morgan as if she had been away from the office for a year instead of six weeks. The work had piled up to the extent that she found herself working through her lunch hours, and going home an hour later than usual in the afternoon in order to catch up. The relief typist had obviously done only what had been absolutely necessary, but the rest of it had been left on Morgan's desk to await her return.

After those lazy days in Rossmere with nothing to do but lie about in the sun, Morgan was suddenly working her fingers almost to the bone. She barely had time to think of herself, let alone Carl, and when at last it was time for her cast to be removed she had been left with no option but to have it seen to during her lunch hour as there was no possibility of taking time off. The specialist was pleased, the bones had healed well, and Morgan was justifiably relieved to be free of that weight she had lugged around with her for so long. Her skin was pale where the cast had shielded it from the sun, but that was the least of her problems at that moment, she realised as she glanced at her watch. She would have to hurry, or she would arrive late at the office, and Richard Kelly had not been in one of his best moods that morning after a lengthy session with a difficult client.

Without the awkward cast on her leg Morgan could at last settle back into her normal routine of driving herself to and from work each day. Her office routine also began to show signs of regaining normality, and when the telephone on her desk rang shrilly one morning she found herself far less inclined to want to take an angry swipe at it.

'Mr Kelly's office, good morning,' she said into the mouthpiece.

'Hi, sweetheart,' that unmistakable American accent drifted across the line, and her heart missed an uncomfortable beat.

'Carl!' she exclaimed in surprise, grateful that he could not see her hands trembling as she clutched the receiver to her ear. 'Where are you telephoning from?' she asked when she could hear unfamiliar sounds in the background.

'Jan Smuts Airport,' he replied briskly. 'I've been in the States these past weeks, and I've only just flown in.'

'Oh,' she said stupidly, wondering why her father had not bothered to tell her that Carl had been away, but then, she supposed, what business was it of hers where Carl was, and for how long.

'What time is your lunch hour?' his voice cut impatiently into her thoughts.

'One o'clock.'

'Have lunch with me, honey?'

'I'd like that,' she said at once, glancing up to see Richard Kelly gesturing from the communicating door that he wished to see her at once.

'I'll pick you up outside your offices at one sharp,' Carl said abruptly. ''Bye for now.'

The line went dead and, thankful that he had not prolonged their conversation, Morgan replaced the receiver and walked quickly into her employer's office.

'I'm looking for the Wheeler v. Carter file,' Richard Kelly told her irritably. 'Do you think you could find it for me?'

Morgan sighed inwardly. This was going to be one of *those* mornings! The girl who had relieved her had obviously filed it incorrectly, as she had done with so many others, and Morgan knew from experience that she could forget about her lunch hour if she did not find that file, and find it quickly.

It was a few minutes to one o'clock when her frantic search was rewarded and, with an audible sigh of relief, she placed the Wheeler v. Carter file on her employer's desk.

'I hope you won't mind if I rush off, but I have a luncheon appointment,' she muttered a little breathlessly, and barely waited for Richard Kelly's approval before she rushed out of his office, snatched up her handbag in passing her desk, and headed towards the lift.

The silver Porsche slid to a halt at the entrance of the building just as Morgan stepped out on to the pavement, and she hurried towards it.

Carl smiled at her briefly when she slipped in beside

him, his glance taking in everything from her hair, twisted into a neat knot at the nape of her neck, down to her shoes, which matched her beige outfit.

'Bless you for being punctual,' he said. 'There's never any parking in these busy streets.'

'I nearly didn't make it,' she laughed breathlessly, hardly able to take her eyes off him. 'Mr Kelly urgently required a case file which had disappeared mysteriously, but it had simply been filed incorrectly, and I was lucky to find it so quickly.'

She had a horrible feeling that she was babbling unnecessarily, but she was nervous and excited, and her heart was beating much too fast for comfort. She knew a crazy desire to touch him, to run her fingers through his short, silver-fair hair, but she fought it down, and clenched her hands tightly in her lap while he drove a few blocks away to a small restaurant she had never been to before.

They both ordered a light lunch, settling for a small sole and a salad, and it was only then that she saw the greyness of his pallor, while fatigue had planted deep grooves from his nose to his mouth. Their eyes met, and she was a little disconcerted to discover that he had been studying her as intently as she had been studying him.

'You're looking good, Morgan,' he said, resting his elbows on the table, and studying her with renewed interest.

'I wish I could say the same about you,' she replied with a measure of concern. 'Has it been an exhausting trip?'

'Yeah,' he drawled grimacingly, brushing a hand over his face. 'I was so busy going over contracts and what-have-you on the plane that I never slept, but now I could certainly do with a couple of hours' shut-eye.'

'Do you have to return to Rossmere this afternoon?'

'Not necessarily, why?' he asked blankly.

Morgan chewed thoughtfully on her bottom lip, and came to a hasty decision. 'Why don't you make use of my flat, and rest a few hours before you attempt the car journey back to Rossmere?'

His eyebrows rose mockingly. 'What will your honourable caretaker have to say when he sees a strange man going into your flat in the middle of the day?'

'He won't say anything,' she smiled encouragingly. 'I'll give him a ring to let him know that you're a friend who's badly in need of a place to rest up for a few hours before you travel further, and that will be that.'

'Well, I . . .'

'Here's the key,' she interrupted what seemed like a refusal and, taking it out of her handbag, she passed it to him across the checkered tablecloth.

'You're sure you don't mind?'

An inexplicable tenderness welled up inside of her. 'You're tired, Carl, and I see no purpose in going into a hotel for an hour or two when you can use my flat.'

'Thanks,' he smiled briefly, his hand covering hers where it lay on the table, and her fingers curled about his of their own volition.

It was crazy, she supposed, but she knew now that she had missed him, and she had longed for his touch, however impersonal it might be. 'Don't fall in love with him,' her father's warning leapt into her mind, and she was wondering how to extricate her hand from Carl's when their lunch was served.

They ate their meal without attempting to make

conversation, but the atmosphere was not uncomfortable. There was, strangely enough, no need to search her mind frantically for something to say, and she found herself relaxing in Carl's company while they enjoyed their lunch in companionable silence.

He looked up when she passed him his coffee, and when his tired eyes met hers, she said: 'You're working too hard.'

'I have to if I want to keep abreast of developments.'

'No human being can cope physically with being in two places at the same time,' she remonstrated with him, 'and that's what you're attempting to do.'

'Are you concerned about me?' he questioned mockingly.

'Naturally I'm concerned about you.'

'Any special reason?'

Her breath caught in her throat when she realised how easily she had walked into that trap, and her cheeks went a delicate shade of pink as she said defensively, 'Wouldn't you be concerned about a friend if you knew he was working himself to a frazzle?'

His eyes, dark and compelling, held hers captive as he leaned towards her across the small table. 'Do you know what I'd like to do this very minute?'

'You'd like to go to sleep,' she clutched nervously at the most logical answer, but he shook his head slowly.

'I'd like to kiss you,' he murmured so that only she could hear, and her cheeks went a much deeper shade of pink.

'Please, Carl,' she protested, lowering her eyes to the checkered tablecloth.

'Is that an invitation?'

'You know it isn't, so behave yourself,' she answered crossly.

'Yes, ma'am.'

She looked up into those mocking blue eyes, and suddenly they were laughing together with a certain intimacy that made her pulse behave quite irrationally.

A few minutes later a quick glance at her watch made her say apologetically, 'I hate to rush you, Carl, but it's almost two o'clock.'

'Come on,' he said, not attempting to detain her, and he held her hand as they walked out of the restaurant, his palm warm and slightly rough against hers.

'When you leave simply slip the key into my post box,' she said when he dropped her off at the office.

'I'll do that, honey,' he smiled briefly. 'See you!'

She stood there for a moment staring after him, then she turned and quickly entered the building. Why did she feel so desolate all at once, as if the warmth had gone out of the day? She thumbed the lift button and sighed, wishing suddenly for something she could not even explain to herself.

Morgan was too busy that afternoon to allow her thoughts to dwell on Carl, and she worked almost without a break until it was time to go home.

'I'll be in late tomorrow morning,' Richard Kelly warned her on their way out of the office. 'I'll be in court until eleven, but I've prepared a brief which I'd like you to type for me. You'll find it on my desk blotter.'

Morgan nodded tiredly, and they parted company moments later when they stepped out of the lift, each going their own direction to where their cars were parked in the basement.

When she arrived home fifteen minutes later she

found her key in the post box as she had requested, and beside her bed, in a slim white vase, there were three long-stemmed pink roses. She stared at them amost in open-mouthed fascination, then she leaned over to inhale their sweet fragrance and to finger the soft, velvety petals. A small white envelope stood propped up against the vase, and her fingers trembled slightly as she lifted the flap to extract the card on which a message had been written in a bold, masculine handwriting.

Lovely lady, your kindness has been appreciated. I'll see you Friday evening, and keep the weekend free for me if you can. Carl.

There was a fluttering in her throat, and her heart was singing out wildly, 'Friday, Friday! I'll see him on Friday!' Oh, God, it was crazy to feel this way; to be so terribly elated at the thought of seeing him again soon. She sat down on the bed and brushed her hand lightly over the pillow where she could still see the indentation of his head, and she felt curiously choked at the thought that he had lain there only a few brief hours ago.

'Don't fall in love with him, Morgan,' she lectured herself sternly as her father might have done. 'He doesn't believe in the things that are important to you. He'll love you now, and break your heart into a thousand pieces tomorrow without thinking twice about it.'

Angry and agitated with herself, she thumped the pillow into shape to wipe out the imprint of Carl's head, but the roses were still there; a tangible, fragrant reminder of his presence and, as she reached out to finger the soft petals, she knew that it was hopelessly too late. She had been caught and fatally trapped in the silken web of his practised charm like an inquisitive fly attracted to a brightly coloured spider, and for her there would be no escape from this prison into which she had plunged herself.

Her insides began to shake. How had it happened? How could she have allowed it to happen? She pulled the pins out of her hair and shook it free, then went through her usual ritual of changing into something more comfortable, and preparing a meal for herself, but her mind was not on what she was doing. When she finally sat down at the counter in the kitchen with her plate of food in front of her, she found that she had no appetite at all and, after forcing herself to take a couple of mouthfuls, she pushed aside her plate and helped herself to a cup of coffee.

Morgan's peaceful evening at home became a nightmare of ebbing and flowing thoughts. 'Be sensible! Think rationally!' she told herself when she crawled into bed much later that night. 'See Carl Ziegler for what he really is; a man who has an interest solely in your body. He couldn't care less about your mind, nor your soul, and once he's taken his fill of your body he'll discard you like an old shoe for which he has no further use. Constancy, where women are concerned, has no place in his life, and you *know* that.'

She sighed and tried to go to sleep, but in her mind she saw Carl's mocking blue eyes observing her beneath straight brows a shade darker than his hair, and the sensually chiselled mouth above the square, determined jaw smiled at her in that bone-melting way.

'You're a tough nut, honey, but I'll crack you yet,' his statement of a few weeks ago rang in her ears, and she turned her face into the pillow with a groan of despair on her lips.

'God help me,' she muttered in a muffled, choked voice, 'I've cracked already, but he must never know it. *Never!*'

When Andrew Field telephoned Morgan on the Thursday evening she prided herself on being completely in charge of herself once more, but this feeling lasted only until her father said: 'There are rumours floating about that the Triton is to become a subsidiary company of Carl's firm in Washington, and that he'll soon be stationing himself there.'

Her heart sank like the mercury in a thermometer on a freezing night. 'You mean he'll be living in America and coming out to South Africa only occasionally?'

'With a good man at the helm of the Triton company there'll be no need for Carl to come out here unless it's absolutely necessary,' he confirmed.

'Oh!' she breathed as the mercury dropped several degrees more to send an icy chill along her veins.

'Nothing is definite yet,' Andrew cautioned. 'The discussions and final decision will have to take place at a board meeting, so it's all still rumours.'

'Of course,' she muttered thickly, feeling as though someone had caught her by the throat and was taking a great delight in strangling her slowly.

'Morgan?'

'Yes?' she croaked.

'You're not upset, are you?'

'Not at all,' she lied, making a desperate attempt to pull herself together, and succeeding partially. 'I've actually been expecting something like this.'

'He told you about his plans?' her father questioned sharply.

'Not exactly,' she replied hurriedly, not wanting to give the wrong impression. 'Carl did happen to mention once that he might not always be travelling back and forth between the two continents the way he had been doing since his arrival in Rossmere.'

'So there could be some truth in those rumours?'

'There could be,' she admitted reluctantly, 'but as Carl always says—don't bet on it.'

'I won't,' her father agreed with a smile in his voice.

They talked for a while longer, but Morgan found it difficult concentrating on the rest of their conversation, and when she eventually put down the receiver she was shivering as if it was midwinter instead of September, when the earth started coming alive again after the cold, frosty months.

So Carl was thinking of returning to America, and if there were rumours to that effect then they must have come from somewhere, but now, at least, she was prepared for it. She would know how to deal with the situation, and herself, in future, and that was something she ought to be grateful for. She had been warned.

Morgan was soaking herself in a hot, scented bath later that evening when the telephone started ringing in the lounge. She decided to ignore it at first, but the caller was nothing if not persistent. Sighing irritably, she stepped out of the bath and wrapped her towel around her wet body while she walked quickly from the bathroom into the lounge.

'Hi, honey,' Carl's voice came over the line when she had lifted the receiver to her ear. 'I knew you were home because I telephoned your father not half an hour ago, and he told me that he had spoken to you earlier this evening.' There was a brief silence while Morgan stood there clutching the receiver as if she had turned to stone, then he asked with a faintly sensuous laugh, 'were you in bed?'

'I was in the bath, and I happen to be dripping water all over the carpet at the moment,' she told him coldly, despite the heavy thumping of her treacherous heart.

'Hm . . . a delightful picture comes to mind.'

The raw sensuality in his voice sent a quiver along her receptive nerves, but she clamped down on her feelings and demanded abruptly, 'What did you want?'

Again there was a brief pause. 'Are you angry about something, honey?'

'No,' she lied, 'but I'd like to get back to my bath.'

'If I were there would you have let me soap your back?'

She felt herself blush from her toes up to the roots of her hair, and her voice was uncommonly sharp when she said: 'Say what you have to say, Carl, or I'll put the receiver down.'

'Sure, sweetheart,' he laughed softly. 'I'll call for you at six-thirty tomorrow evening, and I've made arrangements for us to dine at a place that apparently has an excellent floor show.'

'You had no right to simply assume that I'd be free to see you tomorrow evening.'

The line seemed to crackle with static electricity before he spoke. 'You got my message, Morgan, and if you weren't free tomorrow evening you would have let me know at once, so, whatever it is that's making you behave so obstinately this evening, it had better be good, because I shall demand an explanation when I see you tomorrow.' His voice was harsh with an anger she had never heard before. 'I'll see you at six-thirty and be ready.'

'Carl, I—*Carl!*' The line went dead before she could finish what she had been about to say and, slamming the receiver back on to its cradle, she muttered furiously, '*Damn!*'

She was shaking all over when she returned to the bathroom. *Damn* Carl Ziegler for having this effect on her! Who the devil did he think he was, and what did he think he was playing at? A sob rose in her throat, but she choked it back. 'Oh, why can't you leave me alone!' she cried out, her voice hollow with anguish, but the four walls of the bathroom remained silent witnesses to her aching misery.

Morgan slept fitfully that night, and she was not in one of her most cheerful moods when she arrived at the office the following morning and sat down behind her typewriter. Richard Kelly dictated letters like a fiend that morning for almost two hours, and before she left his office he thrust a cassette tape into her hand.

'I recorded my notes on the Jacobs case, and I'd like them typed and filed before you go home this afternoon,' he instructed, putting on his jacket and picking up his briefcase. 'I shall be in court for the rest of the day, if anyone should enquire, and if there are any messages, leave them on my desk.'

He marched out of the office, leaving Morgan with a pile of work which could quite easily mean that she would have to work through her lunch hour if she hoped to have it all finished before five that afternoon, but she was more grateful than angry when she sat down behind her desk and thrust the first sheets of paper and carbon into the typewriter.

Her fingers pounded away at the keys, leaving her no time to think, or feel, as the day progressed, and she was tired but satisfied when she pulled the cover over the typewriter late that afternoon. Despite all the telephone interruptions, and the queries which she had had to deal with, there was a neat pile of letters on her employer's desk awaiting his signature, and his notes on the Jacobs case had been typed and filed for his inspection in the morning. She could go home at last, but her smile of pleasure vanished at the thought of what lay ahead of her.

A few evenings ago she had looked forward elatedly to seeing Carl again, but now she shrank from the thought. If she did not take care he would bend her to his will as easily as one might bend a sapling, and it was this knowledge that frightened her most. She was not a coward, in normal circumstances, but she knew when she was up against something which she could not cope with, and Carl Ziegler was that *something* that immovable object which seemed to be intent upon destroying her peace of mind.

When her doorbell rang at six-thirty sharp that evening, Morgan felt a shiver of apprehension race along her spine, and she muttered a little prayer for help as she walked stiffly across the lounge towards the door . . . and opened it. Carl stood there, the height and breadth of him filling the doorway, and his dark impeccably tailored evening suit lending a formidable air to his already imposing appearance.

'Hi, gorgeous,' he said with a smile in his voice, but that smile was not mirrored in those hooded eyes that swept her from head to foot.

'Hello, Carl,' she greeted him with a calmness she was far from experiencing as she stepped aside for him to enter.

'The last time we met I found myself thinking we were getting along like a house on fire,' he remarked when she had closed the door and they stood facing each other in her bright but cheaply furnished lounge. 'What happened between then and now to change you into a cool, aloof young lady once more?'

'I've come to my senses,' the words hovered on her lips, but instead she said bluntly, 'Nothing happened.'

'Come off it, Morgan,' he ordered harshly, his hands biting unexpectedly into her shoulders, forcing her to face him when she would have turned away. 'One day you give me the friendly come on, but not a week later you give me the brush-off. I think I'm entitled to know why, and I'm demanding an explanation.'

His eyes were no longer lazy, but blazingly intent upon her face, and she looked away from him, afraid of what he might see.

'Why me, Carl?' she asked unsteadily, still not able to look at him. 'There are so many women who would be only too willing to comply with your demands, yet you choose someone who's not interested in the fleeting entanglements you're searching for.'

'You're beautiful, Morgan.'

'I'm not,' she snapped angrily, brushing his hands off her shoulders and turning away from him. 'My mouth is too big, and my nose is too small.'

'I like you just the way you are.'

'Oh, I'm sure you do,' she replied sarcastically.

His hands were on her hips, drawing her back against his hard body, and his warm, sensual mouth trailed a path of fire across her bare shoulder that sent a spate of pleasurable sensations rippling through her.

'You're also very desirable,' he murmured against

her throat, his hands sliding possessively across her stomach.

'Only because I'm unobtainable,' she argued in a voice that sounded abominably faint as she fought against the longing that was like an ache deep down inside of her.

'I can't accept or believe that you're so totally unwilling,' he grunted, taking her by the shoulders and swinging her roughly round to face him.

'I've said it once before, Carl, and I'll say it again,' she bit out the words as she bravely met the shattering onslaught of his eyes. 'Nothing on earth will induce me to go to bed with you simply for the sake of providing you with a few hours of passion!'

'I want more from you than that.'

'Such as?' she demanded suspiciously, neither expecting nor hoping for anything permanent.

'I'm working on it,' he smiled mockingly.

'You're wasting your time,' she told him crossly, trying to break free of those hands which slid down her back to draw her so relentlessly towards him.

'I'll decide that for myself.'

'Oh, for heaven's sake!' she exploded, her hands flat against his hard chest in a futile attempt to ward him off. 'Why won't you believe that I'm not your type?'

'Because you're very much my type, honey, only you're too stubborn to see it,' he laughed cynically, trapping her slim softness helplessly in his arms.

His mouth swooped down on to hers, giving her no opportunity to avoid his kiss, but she remained passive in his arms with her lips tightly pressed together in an attempt not to respond. Carl was in no hurry to release her, she soon discovered. He took his time, equally determined to break down her resistance as she was to uphold it, and he succeeded in a diabolically clever way. He forced her backwards over his arms, leaving her no option but to cling to his shoulders for support, and making her so intensely aware of the dominance and need of his hard male body that the shock of it vibrated through her and shattered her resistance. She yielded against him until her womanly softness was crushed against rock-hard hips and thighs. Her lips parted of their own volition beneath the insistent pressure of his, and then she was lost in the ever widening whirlpool of her emotions. With one hand still clamped firmly against the hollow of her back, he slid the other upwards in a leisurely caress from her thigh to clasp her breast through the peach-coloured silk of her dress, and—God help her—she was doing nothing at all to stop him.

The sensual pressure of his caressing fingers sent a shudder of the most incredible desire through her, and when he finally eased his mouth from hers she found herself clinging to the lapels of his jacket like someone in a drunken stupor. His hands were clamped about her waist, giving her the necessary support while her legs felt as if they would cave in beneath her, and several seconds passed before she found that she could breathe and think normally again.

She moved away from him jerkily at last to press her hands against her flushed cheeks. 'You shouldn't have done that, Carl.'

'Why not?'

'If you expect me to spend the evening with you, then I must ask you to behave yourself,' she replied, regaining her composure painfully and slowly.

'I'll behave myself, but I shan't promise not to kiss you again,' he warned, picking up her wrap and draping it carefully about her shoulders, then he thrust her evening bag into her hands and said calmly, 'Shall we go?'

His hand supported her beneath her elbow as they walked from her flat into the lift. His touch was proprietorial and conveyed his undeniable confidence in himself, or was it simply a display of arrogance? He had won this round without much effort, but she was determined that he would not win the next. She still had some fight left in her, and soon he would discover this.

CHAPTER FIVE

THE restaurant Carl took Morgan to that evening was filled to capacity, and she suspected that the superb cuisine was only one of many reasons why couples who had not made a booking had to be turned away at the door. Diners could enjoy their meal while watching the excellent floor show, and a space had been cleared for those who wished to dance during those moments in between performances.

It was on one such an occasion that Carl took Morgan's hand and urged her on to the floor, and when he took her into his arms she felt again the shock of his body against her own. The music was slow and dreamy, and Carl was an excellent dancer, but his lips brushing against her hair and his hard thighs moving against her own were too much for her to bear.

'Must you hold me so tight?' she complained eventually, straining against the immovable steel of his hand against the hollow of her back.

'I like to feel your body moving against mine.'

There was something crudely sexual in his statement, and she caught her breath sharply. 'I'm not going to argue with you, but I would prefer not to be held so tightly, if you don't mind.'

His arm relaxed about her, allowing a little space to come between them, and when she happened to look up at him she found him frowning down at her.

'You've been sparring verbally with me all evening,

and keeping me at arm's length,' he growled.

'Any girl in her right mind would do that,' Morgan told him coldy, and his lips twisted cynically.

'The big bad wolf, huh?'

She lowered her eyes to concentrate on the knot in his black silk tie. 'You've given me no reason to believe otherwise.'

'Haven't I?' he demanded, pulling her up against him and swaying backwards to avoid a collision with a couple prancing wildly across the floor.

'No, you haven't,' she persisted, breathing a little easier when he slackened his hold once more.

'Haven't I been remarkably patient with you?'

'Patient, yes ... but your ultimate aim remains the same.'

'I'm a man, honey, not a saint,' he laughed softly close to her ear. 'Show me a man who doesn't get ideas when he sees a beautiful woman, and I'll show you a fossilised human being.'

Morgan did not reply to that, but when the music ended, the numb pain in her right calf forced her to say, 'Could we sit out the next dance, do you think?'

'Sure,' he agreed at once, his rapier-sharp glances glimpsing that flicker of pain on her face as he linked her arm through his. 'Does your leg ache?'

'A little,' she confessed as they returned to their table. 'It's been a long time since I've indulged in so much dancing.'

'I'm sorry, honey,' he murmured with touching concern, bending over her chair to make sure she was seated comfortably. 'I didn't mean to tire you.'

'Tell me about your last trip to the U.S.A.,' she changed the subject when he had seated himself opposite her. 'Did you have time to visit your ranch?'

'There wasn't time to go out to Wyoming, I'm afraid.' He gestured vaguely and sighed. 'Maybe next time.'

'Were you terribly busy?' she asked, deciding it was a safe topic to stick to.

'Terribly,' he echoed, frowning down at the table-cloth. 'I worked days, and quite often nights as well.'

'How long do you think you're going to be able to keep up the pace?'

'Only as long as I have to.'

The conversation she had had with her father leapt into her mind, and she asked cautiously, 'Are you considering making a few changes?'

'I don't want to talk business when I'm with you,' he said abruptly, his mouth tightening perceptibly, and she felt her back go rigid with distaste.

'Do you consider I don't possess the mental capacity to understand?'

'I think you're a beautiful and very intelligent young woman,' he sighed, a hint of irritation in his deep voice, 'but right now I want to forget about work and the problems arising from it.'

The candle flickered between them on the table, cruelly accentuating the lines of strain on his face, and that inexplicable tenderness swept through her again.

'I'm sorry,' she heard herself whispering apologetically.

The mood of the evening altered abruptly. Morgan relaxed for the first time, and they drifted into a light hearted conversation that eased that peculiar tension which had hovered between them. They left the restaurant later that evening, shortly after a male vocalist had grunted his way through a love song, and Morgan was feeling pleasantly tired when they arrived at her flat.

She made coffee and they drank it in the lounge where Carl sat sprawled on the sofa. Morgan had kicked off her shoes and sat curled up in the chair facing him, but when she got up to place her empty cup in the tray, his fingers snaked about her wrist, and she was pulled down on to the sofa beside him.

He stared down into her wary eyes and smiled mockingly. 'You still remind me of biscuits and cheese—fragile, spicy, and quite delectable.'

Play it cool, she warned herself, and without averting her eyes from his, she said: 'The way you say that makes me think I shall need to defend myself shortly.'

'You may not want to defend yourself,' he warned her with a devilish gleam in his eyes as they roamed the delicate contours of her features.

'As a self-confessed seducer of women you would know exactly how to deal with any form of resistance,' she replied, recalling only too vividly how he had broken down the rigid barriers she had erected earlier that evening. 'While I'm still in complete control of all my faculties, however, I must warn you that I'm very unwilling to be seduced.'

'Don't you like me?'

He adopted an expression that made him look very much like a pathetic little boy, something which she was certain he had never been, and she could not prevent the laughter that bubbled past her lips. 'Oh, Carl, of course I like you, but I've told you this before—I'm old-fashioned.'

He leaned towards her purposefully. 'I'm tempted to reform you.'

'Oh, dear, and here I was hoping we could still be friends,' she remarked airily, determined not to take him seriously.

'It's natural for friendships to ripen into something more cosy,' he explained, and the blatant sensuality in his deep voice brought a cynical smile to her lips.

'Such as a frolic in bed?' she asked bluntly.

He flicked her cheek with a lazy finger. 'You have a one-track mind.'

'When I'm with you that's hardly surprising.'

She could have bitten off her tongue the next instant, and her face went hot as he laughed that soft, deep-throated laugh and said mockingly, 'I adore you when you blush.'

'You have that effect on me sometimes,' Morgan tried to salvage what was left of her crumbling composure.

'Only sometimes?' he demanded with a sly grin, his eyes appraising her with a deliberate slowness from head to foot until she felt hot and flustered.

'Stop it, Carl,' she ordered huskily, 'and don't look at me like that!'

'Like what?' he asked without taking his eyes off the enchanting curve of her breasts which were beginning to rise and fall agitatedly under his sensually disturbing surveillance.

'You're looking at me in a way that—that makes me feel quite—quite undressed,' she stammered annoyingly, her nerves quivering in response to his nearness.

'You're wearing a beautiful dress, but you would be equally beautiful without it, and your skin would be——'

'Shut up!' she hissed in alarm, her colour rising

sharply, and her heart behaving like a wild bird in a cage. 'I'm not made of stone, Carl. I'm flesh and blood, and what you're saying is positively indecent!'

'Why?' he demanded softly, his voice like a physical caress against exposed, receptive nerves. 'Do you consider sex indecent?'

Morgan caught her breath sharply, and leapt to her feet. She had endured enough, her senses had been stimulated to breaking point, but she would not allow it to continue and, staring down at him coldly, she said: 'Thank you for a delightful dinner as well as a most entertaining evening.'

'If I had a hat then that would be my cue to pick it up and leave,' he laughed, raising his arms and locking his hands behind his fair head in a way that parted his jacket to make her aware of the play of muscles in his broad chest beneath the tight span of his white silk shirt. 'I'm sorry to disappoint you, honey, but I'm not going to leave just yet.'

She clenched her shaking hands at her sides, and wished suddenly that she had not taken off her shoes when she saw his glance slide down to her stockinged feet. 'I won't change my mind, you know, and just think how undignified it would be if we had to indulge in a brawl while you forced me to give in to you.'

Carl's eyes flickered dangerously. 'Don't put ideas into my head.'

'That would hardly be necessary,' she retorted stiffly. 'Your head is crammed so full of ideas where women are concerned that I doubt if there's room for one more.'

He laughed loudly at that, white teeth flashing against his tanned complexion, then he lunged forward unexpectedly, and his fingers snaked about her wrist before she had time to move out of reach. She tried to jerk herself free, but his fingers merely tightened about her wrist, and she was pulled roughly down into his arms so that she found herself lying partially in his lap.

'I know I've said it before, but you're absolutely unique,' he said, laughter glinting in his eyes as he observed her frantic efforts to free herself.

'You find me unique because I refuse to fall into bed with you like a meek little lamb, is that it?' she demanded breathlessly.

'For that reason,' he admitted, 'and quite a few others, but you might as well get used to the idea that I'm going to make love to you in the not too distant future, and there'll be no need to indulge in an undignified brawl, because you'll want it as much as I do.'

His lips against hers silenced her repudiating remarks, and during the next few minutes Morgan was made frighteningly aware of how little resistance she actually had against a man of his experience. The sensual warmth of his mouth was like a potent drug sapping her strength, and it ignited a strange fire in her body. His fingers were against her scalp, scattering the pins so that her hair tumbled in a red-brown cloud about her face. He caressed her throat, her shoulders, and finally ventured beneath the pencil-thin straps of her dress. She felt something give way, and felt the coolness of air against her body, but she had reached the stage where she neither knew nor cared what was happening. His hands had gained access to her breasts, his fingers probing and caressing, and she moaned against his lips, locking her arms about his neck as a shudder of desire shot through her.

Morgan was lost, caught up in the storm of passionate desire that swept through her like an alien force against which she had no protection. Carl's mouth was like fire against her skin as it trailed across her throat, then his mouth dipped lower to her breast, and her breath came jerkily over her parted lips.

'Oh, Carl, *Carl*!' she breathed his name in ecstasy as his tongue made lazy, erotic circles round the swollen peak of her breasts before taking it into his mouth, and suddenly her body was pulsating with a need so intense that it was a physical pain.

His mouth sought hers again, and he kissed her hungrily as if he were drinking nectar from her lips until she was no longer conscious of anything except the surprising softness of his hair beneath her fingers when she shamelessly guided his hungry mouth down to her breast once more. She felt him shudder against her, and felt the almost convulsive tightening of his arms about her as he crushed her to him, then he released her abruptly and, breathing heavily, sat staring down into questioning eyes which had become stormy with the passion he had aroused.

With his warmth no longer there to shield her, the cool air rushed up against her to bring her back to her senses, and only then did she realise what had happened. She was lying full-length on the sofa with Carl seated beside her. His heavy-lidded eyes slid over her in a caress, and she was horrified to discover that the bodice of her dress had been pulled down to her waist. Shame burned like acid deep into her soul and, covering herself hastily, she scrambled to her feet with a choked cry on her lips. She was almost feverish in her attempts to restore some order to her appearance, but she was shaking in every limb, and her zip chose this moment to be obstinate.

'Let me,' Carl said roughly behind her, and she was zipped into her dress before she could utter a protest.

He touched her shoulder in an attempt to turn her to face him, but she jerked herself free as every humiliating detail of what had occurred suddenly leapt to the surface of her mind and, mortified, she buried her face in her hands.

'Oh, my God!' she croaked in a muffled, disgusted voice. 'All my glib talk has amounted to nothing. You could have had me just now, and I wouldn't have stopped you.'

'Morgan . . .'

'Why didn't you take me?' she demanded incredulously, her voice tinged with sarcasm as she scraped together sufficient courage to turn and face him. 'Just think how you could have gloated afterwards as a result of your easy victory!'

'You said I would know how to deal with any form of resistance—well, perhaps I do,' he admitted with surprising gravity. 'You also said that you were unwilling for me to make love to you while you were in complete control of your faculties, and that is what stopped me. I want you, Morgan.' The desire smouldering in his eyes confirmed that. 'I want you badly, but for the first time in my life I find myself wanting a woman's mind as well as her body, and I won't make love to you unless you stand there with all your faculties intact and tell me you're willing.'

A mixture of cynical disbelief and suspicion was

mirrored in her eyes. 'Is this some new angle of approach?'

'It's not a new approach, and neither is it a form of persuasion,' he stared grimly. 'It's the simple truth.'

Oh, God, I love this man, she thought as she searched his handsome face and found nothing but grim sincerity there, then she lowered her eyes nervously and, taking a deep breath, whispered, 'I believe you really mean that.'

'I mean it,' he said, taking her hot face between his hands, then he lowered his head and brushed his lips lightly against hers. 'I'll see you tomorrow.'

When he closed the door behind him moments later the latch snapped into place automatically, and the sound of it jarred against her raw, sensitive nerves.

It was a long time before her mind gave her sufficient opportunity to fall asleep that night. Vivid visions of her passionate surrender taunted her until she was bathed in a fiery shame. What on earth had possessed her? And what, in heaven's name, must Carl think of her?

'*But I love him!*' the cry was wrenched from her, and only in that did she find a degree of solace and comfort.

Morgan found a blue airmail envelope jutting out from beneath the sofa the following morning. It contained a bulky letter, and the envelope was addressed to Carl in what looked suspiciously like a feminine handwriting. She flipped the letter in her hand and read the name on the flap. *T. Grayson.* Who was T. Grayson? One of his mistresses from the past, or was she perhaps someone who was still very much in the present?

Morgan fingered the flimsy envelope, tempted to read its contents, but she was disgusted with herself for entertaining such a thought even for a fleeting moment, and she flicked the envelope with its contents intact into the drawer of her small writing desk.

She ate a slice of toast and drank a cup of coffee while she wrote out her shopping list, but her glance travelled repeatedly towards the drawer of her desk. Was it an impassioned love letter from some demented female who had lost her heart to this man who had no use for it? Morgan held the pencil so tightly between her fingers that it almost snapped. Was that not what she had become? She was not demented *yet*, but she had given her heart to a man whose only interest was in her body. *Heaven help me,* she thought despairingly, brushing away a thick strand of titian-coloured hair that had fallen across her face. She had been a crazy, idiotic fool! Her father had warned her; her own common sense had warned her, but she had walked right into the silken web Carl Ziegler had spun, and last night . . .!

Her pencil clattered on to the counter as she buried her hot face in her hands. She did not want to think of last night. It was something she desperately wanted to forget, but her mind was like a demon bent on destruction, and she squirmed inwardly with renewed shame. She had never lost her head like that before. Men had held her hand and kissed her on the lips, but she had never allowed nor wanted them to trespass beyond that, and she had always been controlled enough to put a stop to their amorous advances before the situation could get out of hand. But with Carl . . . oh, God . . . he had simply swept aside her rigid principles, and she had been a willing and eager participant in his game of love. She shuddered now to think of what might have happened had Carl not maintained such a tight leash on his desire, and she had to make sure, somehow, that a similar incident did not occur in future.

Morgan went to town a little later than usual that Saturday morning, and as a result it was difficult, at first, to find parking. Her shopping list was long, and her shoes were pinching her unmercifully when she eventually made her way back to her car. It was twelve-fifteen when she parked her Mini in the basement of the flats, and she was labouring under the weight of her purchases when Carl appeared as if from nowhere at her side.

'Let me help you.'

'Thanks,' she managed unsteadily, relinquishing some of her parcels, but she could not bear looking at him when the lift doors slid shut and closeted them together for a few minutes in the confined space of the air-conditioned cage.

Seeing him again brought the incidents of the previous evening sharply into focus, and she cringed inwardly as the image of his fair head against her breast leapt unbidden into her mind. She felt hot and embarrassed, and aware of Carl's virile presence with every fibre of her being. She felt his eyes on her, willing her to look at him, but she could not; she *dared* not! She was afraid of his mockery, but most of all she was afraid of what *she* might let him see in an unguarded moment.

'I thought we might go out for a drive and have lunch somewhere,' Carl suggested when he deposited her parcels on the counter in her small kitchen. 'I've also made arrangements for us to have dinner at my hotel this evening.'

Morgan kicked off her shoes and leaned tiredly against the cupboard, praying silently for the composure she so desperately needed. 'What about having lunch here and going out afterwards?'

'That sounds even better.' His hands were on her shoulders, turning her to face him, but when she still refused to look at him he placed his fingers beneath her chin and tipped her face up, forcing her to meet his piercing glance. 'Did I put those dark smudges under your eyes?'

Nothing escaped those deceptively lazy eyes, she realised as she brushed aside his query with a casual, 'I didn't sleep very well.'

'Neither did I,' he said roughly, his eyes holding hers captive while his fingers trailed a light caress across her flushed cheek and down the column of her throat to where her pulse was beating so erratically. 'I couldn't stop thinking about you.'

'Don't, Carl ... *please!*' she begged, her colour deepening as she recalled the intimacies she had allowed.

'It's the truth, so help me,' he insisted quietly.

'I can imagine what you must think of me.'

'I think you're very lovely.' His eyes darkened with a hunger that frightened her as he groaned, 'And I want you very much.'

Morgan was conscious of a quivering tautness in his tall, muscled body so close to her own, and her senses responded wildly to the magnetism he exuded. She swayed towards him, reaching out blindly, then she broke free of his spell, and put the length of the small kitchen between them.

'I'd better see to the lunch,' she said, unpacking her parcels, and slamming cupboard doors with unnecessary violence.

She felt his eyes on her as she moved about the kitchen, then he sauntered out into the lounge and made himself at home in front of her hi-fi. She whipped up omelettes and a salad to Helen Reddy singing—*Leave me alone, won't you leave me alone, please leave me alone now, leave me alone!*—Dear God, Morgan thought, if only Carl had left her alone right from the start! It was too late now to say, *leave me alone*—or was it?

Morgan served their lunch on trays in the lounge, and when she got up to pour their coffee she remembered the letter in her writing desk.

'This belongs to you,' she said, taking it out of the drawer and handing it to him.

'Where did you find it?' he asked, staring at the letter in his hand with raised eyebrows.

'It was lying under the sofa this morning,' she told him as she handed him his coffee.

'Did you read it?'

'I'm not in the habit of reading letters that are not addressed to me,' she retorted with a measure of distaste, 'but it's obvious that it's from a woman, and she must be someone special for you to have kept the letter.'

He slipped it into the inside pocket of his jacket and smiled faintly. 'Tammy is someone rather special.'

So it was *Tammy*! Dammit, why did it have to hurt so much!

'You visit her, I suppose, on your frequent trips to Washington?' she twisted the sword in her own heart.

What made Marge burn the toast and miss her favorite soap opera?
A Contemporary Love Story
LOVE BEYOND DESIRE
RACHEL PALMER
...At his touch, her body felt a familiar wild stirring, but she struggled to resist it. This is not love, she thought bitterly.

A SUPERROMANCE™
the great new romantic novel she never wanted to end. And it can be yours

FREE!

She never wanted it to end. And neither will you. From the moment you begin... *Love Beyond Desire,* your **FREE** introduction to the newest series of bestseller romance novels, **SUPERROMANCES**.

You'll be enthralled by this powerful love story... from the moment Robin meets the dark, handsome Carlos ar finds herself involved in the jealousies, bitterness ar secret passions of the Lopez family. Where her own forbidden love threatens to shatter her life.

Your FREE *Love Beyond Desire* is only the beginning. A subscription to **SUPERROMANCES** let you look forward to a long love affair. Month after mon you'll receive four love stories of heroic dimension. Novels that will involve you in spellbinding intrigue, forbidden love and fiery passions.

You'll begin this series of sensuous, exciting contemporary novels... written by some of the top romance novelists of the day... with four each month

And this big value... each novel, almost 400 pages of compelling reading... is yours for only $2.5 book. Hours of entertainment for so little. Far less th a first-run movie or Pay-TV. Newly published novels, with beautifully illustrated covers, filled with page af page of delicious escape into a world of romantic love... delivered right to your home.

A compelling love story of mystery and intrigue... conflicts and jealousies... and a forbidden love that threatens to shatter the lives of all involved with the aristocratic Lopez family.

Mail this card today for your FREE gifts.

TAKE THIS BOOK
AND TOTE BAG FREE!

Mail to: SUPERROMANCE
649 Ontario Street, Stratford, Ontario N5A 6W2

YES, please send me FREE and without any obligation, my **SUPERROMANCE** novel, *Love Beyond Desire*. If you do not hear from me after I have examined my FREE book, please send me the 4 new **SUPERROMANCE** books every month as soon as they come off the press. I understand that I will be billed only $2.50 per book (total $10.00). There are no shipping and handling or any other hidden charges. There is no minimum number of books that I have to purchase. In fact, I may cancel this arrangement at any time. *Love Beyond Desire* and the tote bag are mine to keep as FREE gifts even if I do not buy any additional books.

CI062

Name   (Please Print)

Address   Apt. No.

City

Province   Postal Code

Signature   (If under 18, parent or guardian must sign.)

This offer is limited to one order per household and not valid to present subscribers. We reserve the right to exercise discretion in granting membership. If price changes are necessary you will be notified. Offer expires August 31, 1983.

Printed in Canada   **SUPERROMANCE**

**EXTRA BONUS
MAIL YOUR ORDER
TODAY AND GET A
FREE TOTE BAG
FROM SUPERROMANCE.**

Mail this card today for your FREE gifts.

Canada Post
021
Postes Canada

'I usually make time to see her, yes.' His eyes raked her mockingly. 'Does it make you jealous to know that?'

'Don't be silly,' she snapped, looking everywhere but at him when she felt a guilty flush stain her cheeks and, picking up the trays, she escaped into the kitchen.

'Shall I help you with the dishes?' Carl's mocking voice followed her, and she clenched her hands tightly on the kitchen sink in a desperate attempt to prevent herself from throwing something at him.

'I'll manage on my own, thanks,' she replied in a cool, controlled voice that didn't seem to belong to her.

Morgan had regained her composure when she returned to the lounge some minutes later, but she could not forget entirely about the letter he carried around with him in his pocket. Not even the excitement of the yacht race at the Hartebeespoort Dam that afternoon could dispel her disquieting thoughts entirely, and when Carl dropped her off at her flat at five-thirty that afternoon to change for her dinner date with him, she found herself hovering somewhere between exhilaration and despondency.

It had to end, this futile relationship with Carl, but her heart cried out for her to say and do nothing until it was almost time for him to return to Rossmere. This one weekend, although it was not idyllic, would have to last a lifetime.

When they sat facing each other across the table in the hotel's restaurant, Carl looked up from his steak and pinned her to her chair with those very blue eyes of his.

'You've been preoccupied since this afternoon.'

'Have I?' she asked evasively.

'Do you think I could have your undivided attention this evening?'

An involuntary smile plucked at the corners of her mouth and, putting down her knife and fork, she said: 'You have it.'

'Great!' he grinned.

'What have you planned for this evening?'

'When we've had dinner we're going some place we can relax and enjoy a good show, and afterwards . . .' He paused effectively, and her pulse rate quickened as her mind leapt to the obvious conclusion. Carl smiled wickedly as if he had read her thoughts, then he added softly, 'Let's wait and see, shall we?'

Devil! she thought, her cheeks flushed with embarrassment. He had done that on purpose, and he had succeeded in making her feel as if she had put ideas into his head, instead of it being the other way round. Oh, he was clever, she thought wryly as she tried to concentrate on her food, but he was not clever enough as far as she was concerned.

The play they went to see was a satire, and it would have been amusing had she not been so intensely aware of Carl's shoulder pressing against hers in the narrow theatre seats. His hand eventually found hers in the darkness, and although her initial reaction was to jerk herself free, she decided against it and left her hand in his warm clasp.

'My place or yours?' he asked when they drove away from the theatre that evening, making her recall that first afternoon he had taken her out to lunch in the country, and she glanced covertly at his handsome profile in the dashboard light.

'You don't ever give up, do you?'

'Just testing,' he replied with an abrupt humour. 'Which is it to be?'

'My place,' she said firmly, 'and I don't mean it the way *you* do.'

She saw the mocking twist of his lips, but he said nothing, and neither did she until they stood outside her door.

'Am I invited in for coffee?' he asked when he had unlocked her door and dropped the keys into her outstretched palm.

'If you promise to leave as soon as you've had your coffee,' she told him warily.

'I promise.'

Morgan made coffee and when she returned to the lounge she found Carl sprawled on the sofa once more as if he belonged there. He had removed his jacket and tie, and he sat up, patting the space beside him invitingly, but she ignored his gesture and placed his cup of coffee on the low table beside him. She had had enough for one night of his disturbing nearness, and she did not want a repetiton of the previous evening.

'Do you enjoy working for an attorney?' Carl questioned her at length.

'It's an interesting job.'

'Is your boss any good?'

'He's a very clever attorney,' she assured him. 'I watched him once in court, and I was relieved afterwards that I wasn't the poor soul in the witness stand, but out of the courtroom he's really quite a nice man.'

Carl's eyes were narrowed and watchful. 'You think a lot of this guy, don't you?'

'I respect and admire Richard very much,' she

replied cautiously, putting her empty cup on the low table beside her chair.

'Do I have a rival?'

Morgan felt her nerves jar, but her expression remained calm. 'It's late, Carl, and I think you should go.'

'You're not going to invite me to stay the night?'

She knew he was teasing, but she could not bear it, and her eyes were more green than grey in that moment as she flashed him an angry glance. 'No, I'm not!'

'Then there's nothing else left for me to do but return to my lonely hotel room,' he sighed mockingly as he got to his feet and picked up his jacket.

'Goodnight, Carl, and thanks for a lovely day,' she said when they reached the door.

He put on his jacket, but, instead of leaving, he pulled her roughly into his arms and kissed her so thoroughly that she was breathless and shaking when he eventually released her.

'Goodnight, honey,' he smiled derisively, and then he was opening the door and closing it firmly behind him, leaving her alone in her flat while she fought down her clamouring emotions.

Morgan went to bed that night with her plans firmly sorted out about the future. She would have a serious discussion with Carl when she saw him the following day, and she only prayed that this time she would succeed in convincing him. Something warned her, however, that it was not going to be as easy as she hoped, but it was late, and she was tired, and her doubts could wait until morning.

She slept as if she had taken a sedative, and the ringing of the telephone woke her at nine o'clock on the Sunday morning. Muttering a silent curse, she stumbled out of bed to answer it, and the sunlight streaming in through the lounge window almost blinded her.

'Good morning, sweetheart,' the deep velvet of Carl's voice jerked her wide awake. 'Put on something comfortable. I'm picking you up in thirty minutes and we're going out on a picnic.'

Morgan dug her bare toes into the carpet. 'But I——'

'No "buts", honey,' he interrupted harshly. 'Just be ready when I call.'

There was a decisive 'click', and the next moment the dialling tone was purring in her ear. She frowned down at her toes without actually seeing them, then she raised her glance and caught a glimpse of her flushed face in the mirror against the wall. Her eyes were still heavy with sleep, and her hair hung about her shoulders in total disarray, but when Carl's instructions finally penetrated, she slammed down the receiver and fled to the bathroom with a smothered cry on her lips.

She could not recall ever showering and dressing in such record time before, but when Carl rang her doorbell a half hour later she was dressed except for the scarf with which she was still tying her hair back. She drew a breathless rush of air into her lungs to steady herself as she checked her appearance, and only then did she go and open the door to let him in.

'Hi,' he said, looking her up and down, and finding obvious pleasure in her slim suppleness clad in white slacks and green sweater, then he was ushering her towards the lift which swept them down to where he had parked his Porsche.

CHAPTER SIX

CARL drove to a picnic spot on the outskirts of Pretoria, and there, on that warm Sunday morning in mid-spring, they spread a blanket beneath the trees. It was peaceful and quiet with not many people about, and it was a perfect setting in which to relax, but Morgan felt like a tightly wound spring which needed only the gentlest prod to snap. Carl seemed to sense her mood, and he did not try to pressurise her in any way. He simply talked quietly about his ranch in the mountain state of Wyoming, and of what he still hoped to achieve there. He told her that the first white man to explore Wyoming had been a fur trapper, and that the first permanent settlements were simply fur trading posts.

'There's plenty to do in Wyoming,' he said, lying on his back with his hands locked behind his head, and his eyes narrowed against the sun filtering through the trees. 'One could go hunting, riding, or hiking, but I prefer the trout fishing. It's exciting as well as relaxing.'

'You sound like a travel agent,' Morgan laughed, her insides unwinding slightly.

'Do I?' He looked faintly surprised. 'I like Wyoming. Some of my happiest years were spent there.'

The hint of nostalgia in his voice made her ask, 'Was that when your mother was still alive?'

'Yeah,' he drawled. 'She was a terrific woman. She gave up the country of her birth, and plenty more besides, for my father, and he——'

'And he what?' Morgan prompted, rolling over on to her stomach and propping herself up on her elbows to watch him closely.

'He cheated on her,' came the harsh reply.

'He had affairs?'

'Plenty,' Carl admitted, his mouth thinning into a hard line.

'Is that why you don't see eye to eye with your father, or is it because you're so like him?'

She held her breath, wondering whether she was prying too deeply into something which did not concern her, but he raised himself up on to one elbow and faced her with a sardonic gleam in his lazy eyes.

'A bit of both, I guess, and that's why I don't believe in marriage,' he answered her query. 'How can I be sure when I commit myself to a woman that I'm going to feel the same in twenty or thirty years from now?'

'That will depend a lot on the woman.'

His eyebrows met in a straight line above narrowed eyes. 'Are you suggesting, by any chance, that my mother drove my father into the arms of all those other women?'

'I wouldn't dare suggest anything of the sort,' she retorted, sitting up abruptly, 'but how much do you know of what went on between your parents when they closed their bedroom door at night?'

'Nothing, of course, but——'

'Then how can you reject marriage and condemn your father without a hearing?' she interrupted sharply.

'I know what he did to my mother,' Carl insisted stubbornly.

'Have you ever tried to find out what she did to him, perhaps?'

'Dammit, Morgan!' Carl roared, his face dark with

anger as he sat up and faced her. 'My mother was a woman in a million!'

'I don't dispute that.'

'Then what are you trying to do?' he demanded harshly, making her shrink inwardly from the angry fire in his eyes. 'Make me hate her?'

She gestured helplessly with her hands and sighed, 'You've misunderstood me.'

'I don't think so.'

'Yes, you have,' she insisted tersely. 'I'm sure your mother was a wonderful woman, but I haven't worked for an attorney for almost three and a half years without learning that there are always two sides to every story.'

An angry silence hovered between them, but before she could formulate some sort of apology in her mind, Carl said: 'Maybe it's time I had a chat with my father.'

'Maybe it is,' Morgan agreed weakly, expelling the air slowly from her lungs.

The hotel had packed them a picnic lunch which was more like a feast. There was chicken, a salad, fresh bread rolls, tiny apple pies, and a bottle of wine chilled between ice packs. After the first glass of wine Morgan felt herself relax, after the second she felt lightheaded and giggly, and after the third she was definitely in the mood to do almost anything. The latter was a dangerous mood to be in when she was with Carl, and she had to remember that. Think sober thoughts and don't relax your guard too much, she told herself as she helped herself to a small apple pie, and slanted a nervous glance at his handsome profile.

'Will you be happy when I'm gone?' Carl asked some time after the effects of the wine and good food had worn off.

'Gone where?' she asked abruptly, a coldness shifting over her heart as she rolled over on to her stomach and plucked nervously at a blade of grass.

'Rossmere, of course,' he smiled faintly.

'Do you want me to say that I didn't enjoy this weekend with you?'

'*Did* you enjoy it?'

This was her opening, the opportunity she had waited for, but she was reluctant to take it as she shrugged and said: 'Yes and no.'

'What does that mean?' he demanded, lying on his back with his hooded eyes fixed intently on her face, and it made her feel decidedly uncomfortable.

'I—I enjoyed the weekend, but I——'

'But you what?' he prompted harshly.

There was no way out of this except by telling the truth, and as the blade of grass snapped between her agitated fingers, she said tritely, 'I don't think we should see each other again.'

The strained silence between them lengthened unbearably, then Carl got to his feet and said bitingly, 'Come on, I'll take you home.'

Morgan felt absolutely wretched as they bundled everything into Carl's Porsche and left. Her mind was in a turmoil; a part of her argued that she had done the right thing, but there was another part that cursed her for being such a fool. Surely it was for the best that they did not see each other again? Nothing could come of this association with Carl . . . only pain . . . and then there was Tammy; Tammy who waited for him in Washington, and whom he made a point of seeing each time he was there. Oh, God, why did it feel as if her very soul was being torn to shreds?

Neither of them spoke until they stood facing each other in the lounge of her flat, and then it was Carl who was demanding harshly, 'Did you mean what you said back there? That you don't think we should see each other again?'

'Yes, I meant it,' she heard herself saying.

'Why?' he bit out the question, his eyes slicing her like lasers.

'Because—because I——'

'Because you're scared?' he finished for her in a derisive voice.

'Scared?' she blinked up at him stupidly.

'Of yourself.'

'You're crazy!' she was almost shouting now as he ventured too close to the truth. 'You're crazy, do you hear me!'

'No, I'm not,' he barked, gripping her shoulders and shaking her. 'You're scared stiff that you might find yourself admitting that you want me.'

She was breathing fast, and her temples were pounding. Anger was her only defence against the truth and, forcing herself to meet the full impact of his furious glance, she snapped, 'Get out of here!'

Carl seemed to go white beneath his tan, then he released her abruptly and snarled savagely, 'With pleasure, ma'am!'

Morgan flinched as he slammed the door behind him, then an oppressive silence descended which was broken only by the painful pounding of her pulses against her temples. She wished it had ended differently; a little more pleasantly perhaps, but she had no doubt that it was to her own advantage not to see Carl again. She swallowed down a couple of aspirins to ease her thumping headache, and she somehow managed to convince herself that the heavy, empty feeling in her chest had nothing at all to do with Carl Ziegler.

Two weeks passed, during which she barely had time to think about herself, let alone someone else, and she was quite often exhausted when she crawled into bed at night. On the Friday morning of the third week she went into Richard Kelly's office as usual to take dictation, and when, an hour later, she closed her notebook and rose to her feet, her employer gestured that she should sit down again.

'I'd like those letters typed and ready for my signature as soon as possible,' he instructed her unnecessarily, almost absentmindedly, and she glanced at him curiously not for the first time that morning.

'Yes, Mr Kelly.'

He dithered a moment and fiddled with the blotter on his desk, then he asked abruptly, 'Are you doing anything special this evening?'

'No,' she replied, smiling faintly. 'Do you want me to work late?'

'I'd like you to have dinner with me.'

'Oh!' she said foolishly, and totally perplexed by this unexpected invitation from her employer.

'I have an important client who prefers to see me at my home rather than here at the office, and I shall need you to take notes,' he explained with a hint of embarrassment in his voice. 'I know this is an unusual procedure, but will you come?'

'Yes, of course,' she replied at once, understanding clearing her brow.

Richard Kelly nodded with satisfaction. 'I'm expecting my client at seven, so I'll pick you up at six, and that should give us plenty of time to prepare for her.'

'*Her?*' Morgan echoed, her eyes widening in surprise. 'Your client is a woman?'

A dull redness surged up into his cheeks. 'That's why I'd like you to be there.'

Morgan rose to her feet and there was a hint of mischief in her eyes when she said: 'I'm at your service.'

A situation such as this had never arisen before, and Morgan found herself feeling amused rather than curious when she returned to her desk. Her employer had invited her to dinner to meet a client, but she suspected that the invitation had been issued for his protection rather than for taking notes, and she found it difficult to suppress the amused smile that continued to tug at the corners of her mouth at odd times during the rest of that day.

Richard Kelly's home was not at all what Morgan had expected. It was furnished with odd pieces of furniture, mostly old, which had been renovated exquisitely for comfort.

'It's a hobby of mine,' Richard explained casually when he glimpsed the curiosity in her glance. 'I buy old pieces of furniture and repair them in my spare time.'

Morgan accepted a glass of wine from him, and changed the subject as she lowered herself into a comfortably padded armchair. 'Am I allowed to know the identity of your client?'

'Does the name De La Rey mean anything to you?' he asked, splashing soda into his whisky before he seated himself in a chair that matched her own to some extent.

'There's a De La Rey who's one of the business

giants in the steel industry,' she replied after a thoughtful pause.

'That's the one.'

'You mean it's his wife?' she grasped the situation at once.

'That's correct,' Richard smiled at the surprise mirrored on her face. 'She wants a divorce, and she wants it done as quietly and discreetly as possible.'

'How quiet and discreet can one keep a divorce when the people involved are so well known?'

He shrugged and swallowed down a mouthful of whisky. 'That depends on what is involved, and how it's handled.'

'You mean if there's no dirty washing to hang out, then there's a reasonable chance of no one knowing until it's all over?' she questioned with faintly cynical interest.

'Something like that,' Richard grinned. 'When the press are excluded from court it shan't even appear in the newspapers.'

They discussed some of the difficult cases he had handled over the years, and Morgan was beginning to wonder what surprises the De La Rey divorce case would spring on them when they heard a car coming up the drive.

Richard went to the door to admit his client personally, and Morgan found herself holding her breath when he ushered the tall, dark-haired woman into the living-room. Morgan had seen Gloria De La Rey's picture many times in the newspapers, but none of those photographs had done justice to her flawless skin and flashing dark eyes, and it was not difficult to see now why she had been judged one of the most beautiful women on the Reef.

'Mrs De La Rey, I'd like you to meet my personal assistant, Morgan Field,' Richard was introducing them, and Morgan only just succeeded in suppressing a smile at the verbal promotion she had received from her employer for the occasion.

'I thought this was going to be a private discussion?' Gloria De La Rey demanded haughtily.

'Morgan can be trusted implicitly,' Richard Kelly assured her hastily.

Those dark eyes looked Morgan up and down with wary scepticism. 'I sincerely hope so.'

Richard's client was nervy and in no mood for the usual pleasantries, and he must have sensed this, for he skipped the ritual of offering her something to drink and said brusquely, 'May I suggest that we sit down to dinner, and discuss the preliminaries to your case while we eat?'

'That suits me perfectly,' Gloria De La Rey announced in her smooth, melodious voice, and Richard helped her slip out of her lightweight coat before he led the way into the dining-room with his client's hand on his arm.

Morgan followed at the rear and realised, with some amusement, that she had not spoken a word since Gloria De La Rey's arrival, but then, she knew, she had not been invited to make bright conversation, merely to listen and take down notes when necessary.

Gloria De La Rey ate sparsely, and her slim figure in that plain but perfectly styled black evening dress was obviously the result of a careful diet. At close quarters her face showed signs of strain, and the fingers that curled about the stem of her wine glass seemed a little shaky when her husband's name was mentioned.

She glanced repeatedly at her diamond-studded wrist watch almost as if she had another appointment for later that evening, and Morgan found herself taking a closer look at this woman who was wanting to instigate divorce proceedings against one of the wealthiest men in the country.

They returned to the living-room after the excellent dinner Richard Kelly had provided, and the information which his client finally gave him was simple and to the point. She had made the discovery recently that her husband had had a brief affair with a young woman in his office. It was, as far as Richard and Morgan could gather, the first time her husband had indulged in an extra-marital relationship with another woman, but Gloria was adamant about not giving him the opportunity to save their marriage. She wanted a divorce, and that was that.

Richard asked the usual questions while Morgan took down notes, and in less than two hours after her arrival Gloria De La Rey was driving away from the house at a speed which made Morgan suspect once again that she was on her way to another engagement.

'You're looking rather pensive?' Richard Kelly remarked when he returned from seeing his client off the premises and found Morgan staring frowningly at the Persian carpet beneath her silver-sandalled feet. 'What are you thinking about so deeply?'

'I was thinking that Mrs De La Rey hasn't told us the entire truth. I have a niggling suspicion that her desire to seek a divorce from her husband is not so much because of his affair with that other woman, but because Mrs De La Rey herself has her eye on someone else.'

'I have that same feeling about her,' Richard observed drily. 'She's hiding something, or protecting someone, and until I know what it is I can't take this case into the courtroom.'

'She'll confide in you eventually,' Morgan reassured him confidently.

'Do you think so?'

'Your clients usually do,' she smiled, putting her notebook and pencil away, and in a hurry suddenly to go home.

'I couldn't tempt you to stay a little longer, I suppose?' he asked, eyeing her speculatively, but she shook her head.

'The dinner was superb, and meeting Gloria De La Rey was an experience I wouldn't have missed, but I must go home now.'

Richard nodded soberly. 'I appreciate the fact that you came at such short notice.'

They did not speak on the way to her flat, and he left her at her door with a curt 'goodnight'. He was a strange man, she thought as she watched him step into the lift, then she turned and inserted her key into the latch.

Morgan's hand found the light switch, but when she turned to close the door behind her it was thrust open with a force that sent her staggering. Her heart leapt into her throat, and fear sent several terrifying thoughts racing through her mind before she recognised the fair-haired man who stood towering over her in the small, dimly-lit entrance.

'Carl!' she breathed his name with a mixture of relief and shocked surprise, but a new kind of fear gripped her when she became aware of his thunderous expression.

'Who's the dude?' he demanded harshly, kicking the door shut and standing so close to her that her nerve ends seemed to vibrate in alarm.

'The who?' she asked confusedly.

'The fancy pants who brought you home,' he explained impatiently.

'That was my boss, Richard Kelly,' she managed when her mind cleared sufficiently for her to grasp what Carl was talking about.

'Are you in love with him?'

She recoiled from him in anger. 'That's none of your business!'

'I'm making it my business!' His hands shot out and gripped her shoulders so tightly that a numb pain shot down into her arms. 'Did he make love to you?'

She might have laughed had she not been so close to tears, but she bit down hard on her lip to steady it. 'You're hurting me!'

'*Did he make love to you?*' he repeated savagely.

'*No!*' she cried hoarsely, and when his hands released her she leaned weakly against the wall to stare up at him in bewilderment. His features were distorted with rage, or something close to it, and he was breathing heavily as if he had indulged in a physical exertion to which he was unaccustomed. 'What's the matter with you, Carl?' she asked at length, wondering if he were not perhaps ill. 'Why are you behaving so strangely?'

'I've been standing around here since seven o'clock this evening waiting for you to come home,' he said accusingly, and she felt her anger return swiftly.

'You surely didn't expect me to sit at home every night, did you? And besides . . .' she led the way into the lounge, '. . . I thought we'd decided not to see each other again.'

'That was your decision, not mine,' he reminded her, taking her by the arm and swinging her round to face him.

'Oh, *Carl*!' she sighed exasperatedly.

His eyes were narrowed to slits of blue fire. 'I can't stay away, honey. Not when I know as well as you do that we've got something going for us.'

Her heart leapt in response, but her mind warned against it. She felt as if she was being torn in two, and she cried out in exasperation and anger, 'For heaven's sake, leave me alone!'

'Dammit, Morgan, will you listen to me?' he thundered.

'No, I will not!'

She tried to break away from him, but he pulled her roughly into his arms, and without any visible effort he subdued her frantic efforts to escape. His hard body against hers ignited a flame within her, and when his mouth touched hers her lips parted of their own volition to respond to his kisses with a hunger she could not suppress nor deny. She melted against him, her body pliant and trembling beneath those clever hands caressing her so freely, but she knew she would despise herself later for having so little strength to fight against the emotions he so successfully aroused. She wanted him, she could admit that to herself, but she did not want him on the basis he had dictated, and for that specific reason she had to hide her true feelings from him—no matter what the cost.

'Look at me now, honey,' he said when at last he raised his head, and his voice was a little unsteady. 'If you can tell me honestly that you felt nothing when I kissed you, then I'll walk out that door and never come back.'

It was difficult to think clearly while she stood in the circle of his arms with the woody scent of his cologne stirring her senses, but she knew she had to answer him with a semblance of truth, if not with complete honesty. 'You're a very attractive man, Carl, and as I've told you before, I'm not made of stone, but——'

'Don't say more than that,' he interrupted softly, his fingers tucking a stray strand of hair behind her ear. 'Let's give ourselves a chance, and see where it all leads.'

I know where it will lead, she thought. You're going to break my heart before you walk away from me, and I shall have no one else to blame but myself.

She should have rejected his suggestion and told him to go, but instead she extricated herself carefully from his arms and said: 'I'll switch on the kettle and make some coffee.'

That was, obviously, enough for Carl. He knew he had won, and Morgan hated herself for allowing him such an easy victory, but she was hopelessly trapped by her own feelings for this man.

She took their coffee through to the lounge some minutes later, and while they drank it she marvelled at how very much alive she felt in Carl's company. She realised now that she had simply existed these past three weeks without his occasional visits, and she was suddenly ridiculously happy that he had not taken her too seriously when she had suggested their not seeing each other again. She was heading towards pain and disillusionment, she warned herself, but for some unknown reason she no longer cared.

'I'm flying to the States on Tuesday,' Carl cut into her thoughts. 'I have business to attend to in Washington, then I'm going out to the ranch in Wyoming for a week or more.' He put his empty cup in the tray and joined her on the sofa. 'Come with me, Morgan?'

Delighted yet shocked at this unexpected invitation, she stared down at the hands that held hers so tightly, and shook her head miserably. 'I can't.'

'Why not?'

'I won't be able to get off from work for one thing and, for another, I don't relish the thought of what people might think and say if it was discovered that I spent some time alone with you on your ranch.'

'For God's sake, Morgan!' he exploded so fiercely that she jumped visibly, then he got to his feet and paced the floor like a furious animal. 'All I want to do is show you around one of the few places where I can unwind from the rigours of work. I'm not inviting you to my ranch for the purpose of seducing you!'

She felt her cheeks grow warm with embarrassment. '*I* know that, and *you* may know it, but there are many who wouldn't believe it was simply an innocent excursion.'

'I'm here now—alone with you in your flat,' he argued harshly. 'If you're so concerned about what people will say, then don't you think we're already making them talk about us?'

She shook her head and forced a smile to her lips. 'You're here, yes, but you'll leave at a respectable hour. If you were seen leaving here in the early hours of the morning, *then* people would have reason to speculate about your presence here.'

He turned abruptly and stared down at her with eyes that were narrowed and intent. 'Your reputation is *that* important to you, is it?'

'I've always lived by certain principles, and I wouldn't enjoy wearing a label I didn't deserve,' she replied with inherent honesty. 'I'm sorry.'

A strained silence lingered in the room for several uncomfortable seconds, and when at last he spoke his voice tripped painfully across the raw edges of her nerves. 'There's nothing more to be said then, is there?'

He turned away from her abruptly, and she sat there staring at the carpet in stunned silence until she heard the door opening. When it clicked shut again she could no longer keep the tears in check. They spilled over on to her cheeks, blinding her, and it was only when she felt the sofa give way beside her that she realised Carl had not left after all.

'Forgive me, Morgan,' his deep voice washed over her soothingly as he pulled her a little roughly into his arms.

'There's nothing to forgive,' she said unsteadily, her voice muffled against his beige jacket.

'I've made you cry.'

'It's only because you don't understand,' she explained, drying her tears with the handkerchief he had placed in her hand.

'I *do* understand,' he said, his fingers caressing her damp, flushed cheek. 'I so desperately wanted to show you my real home in Wyoming, and I wanted to share its beauty with you. I was disappointed when you refused, and because of it I behaved like a stupid idiot.'

'Carl, I——'

'Don't say anything, honey,' he silenced her with his fingers against her lips, then he pocketed his handkerchief and lowered his mouth on to hers.

His kiss was warm and gentle, soothing away the hurt, but passion slipped in unnoticed, and its fire seemed to consume them both. His fingers trailed a sensual path down the hollow of her back as he undid the zip of her evening dress, and her body was achingly eager for his touch when his hands cupped her breasts. His fingers probed and caressed until her body came alive to his touch to leave her quivering and taut with desire. She felt the heat of his mouth against her throat, her shoulder, and the scented hollow between her breasts, and only then did she surface sufficiently from her drugged, happy state to realise what she was allowing once again.

'I—I think you—you'd better go,' she managed haltingly, her breath shallow as she clung desperately to her sanity while every nerve and sinew in her body was crying out with the aching need for the rapture of fulfilment.

'I wish I didn't have to go,' Carl murmured thickly, his mouth against the hollow of her throat where her pulse beat out a pagan rhythm. 'I'd much rather stay here with you, to hold you in my arms, to touch you, and to feel your heart beating against my lips.'

'Please, Carl, I——'

His mouth shifted over hers, silencing her protests, and she was lost for a time, her arms locked about his neck as she responded with a fire of her own to his passionate kisses and wild caresses. It would be so easy to surrender, she realised. So *very* easy. The only thing that held her back was the sure knowledge that she would find it difficult living with her conscience afterwards. She had always secretly despised many of her friends for having so little control over their emotions, but she could no longer despise them; not when she was having such difficulty in controlling her own. She was allowing Carl to caress her with an intimacy she had always denied to others, and the temptation to give herself completely was intensely strong. Her body craved satisfaction, but she knew that her heart, her mind, and her soul would remain untouched if she surrendered herself. In the giving of her body, she would be giving her all, but if Carl could not do the same then she wanted no part of him.

Carl seemed to sense her sudden withdrawal, and he eased himself away from her. His eyes were dark with desire, and his voice was rough with the effort to control himself when he said: 'I've never wanted anyone as much as I want you, Morgan, and that's the gospel truth.'

She ought to have felt flattered, but instead she found herself wondering how many women he had said those exact words to in the past. She escaped from his arms and managed to restore a certain amount of order to her appearance, and only then could she bear meeting those eyes that were watching her so intently.

'I really think you ought to go now,' she managed somehow without a tremor in her voice.

'Do you realise that I shan't be seeing you again until I return from the States?' he demanded, and she was surprised to see his hands shaking when he pushed his fingers agitatedly through his silvery hair.

'You're going back to Rossmere tomorrow?'

'I'm going back tonight.'

Morgan leaned back weakly against the sofa and stared at him in complete bewilderment. 'You mean the only reason you came through to Pretoria this evening was to see me?'

'I was hoping I could persuade you to go to the States with me,' he smiled ruefully, and she lowered her eyes hastily to hide her feelings.

'I'm sorry.'

'So am I.' He got to his feet and drew her up with him, then he looked down into her eyes searchingly. 'Are you going to miss me?'

'I'll do my best,' she teased, but in her heart she knew that she was going to miss him very much.

She walked with him to the door and opened it, but Carl lingered with a reluctance that matched her own. He took her chin between his fingers and raised her face to his.

'About Tammy Grayson,' he said, referring to the letter she had found, and she felt herself go rigid. How could she have forgotten Tammy Grayson? 'Tammy's my sister, she's married, and I have two lively young newphews who drive me crazy at times when Tammy brings them out to the ranch.'

Before Morgan could surface from her shocked surprise he had kissed her fiercely on the lips, and had closed the door behind him.

His sister! The words echoed repeatedly through her mind, mocking her, and quite suddenly she was laughing until there were tears in her eyes. *His sister!* Oh, if only she had known this before, then she might not have behaved as she had done that weekend he had spent here in Pretoria, but it was too late now, and she would not see him again for at least three weeks: three endless weeks during which anything could happen. He could meet someone else—he might even decide not to return, and ... 'Oh, God,' she found herself praying softly. 'Please help me. *Please!*'

CHAPTER SEVEN

'I'M seeing Mrs De La Rey again this evening,' Richard Kelly told Morgan on the following Friday afternoon. 'But this time she insists on seeing me alone.'

'Perhaps it's better that way,' Morgan agreed readily. 'She might give you the information she withheld from you the other evening.'

'I sincerely hope so, because I can't work on the scraps of information I already have.' He frowned at her thoughtfully from the communicating door. 'Did you type the notes you took down that evening?'

'They're in Mrs De La Rey's file,' she told him, pushing back her chair. 'Shall I bring it through to you?'

'Please,' he nodded curtly. 'I'd like to go through them again before I see her this evening.'

Morgan placed the file on his desk a few moments later, and returned to her own desk, but several minutes elapsed before she was able to concentrate on her work once more. What, she wondered, would this second meeting with his beautiful client reveal? Several possibilities came to mind, but Morgan knew the futility of speculation in these matters. She would simply have to wait and see.

She was not looking forward to the weekend ahead of her. The previous weekend had seemed endless, and she felt certain that this one was going to be much worse. She was missing Carl, more than she had thought possible, and if she felt like this after only one week, then how was she going to feel in another three weeks from now? *Terrible*! she answered her own question with a grimace. She would have to keep herself occupied, and not give herself much time to think, but that was rather difficult over a weekend when there was so little to do.

The traffic was heavy late that afternoon when she went home to her flat, and it was with considerable relief that she finally parked her car in the basement garage of the building. She made herself something to eat, listened to records for a while, and eventually went to bed, but her thoughts wandered, and her last waking thought was of Carl. What was he doing? Was he thinking of her? Was he missing her as much as she was missing him?

Morgan filled her Saturday with shopping for supplies and seeing to her clothes, but she dreaded the Sunday most of all. She went out for a drive in her Mini, but wherever she looked people were together in family groups, or pairs, and it increased that feeling of loneliness. It was ridiculous that her entire existence could depend so much on one man, and it was time she pulled herself together, she severely reprimanded herself.

She was intensely relieved when the Sunday drew to a close, and when she went to bed that night she actually looked forward to the following day, and the work which would be waiting for her on her desk. Working for Richard Kelly was stimulating, if nothing else, and her mind was usually fully occupied with legal matters and the updating of files on the various cases her employer handled.

The persistent ringing of the telephone disturbed her during the night, and she switched on the bedside light as she stumbled sleepily out of bed. *Four o'clock!* Could there be something wrong with her father? It was a frightening thought, and she was wide awake now as she pulled on her robe and stormed barefoot into the lounge.

'Hi, honey,' a faint but familiar voice greeted her.

'Carl!' she gasped, relieved and a little angry. 'Do you realise that it's four o'clock in the morning here in South Africa?'

'I know, but I was lying here in bed thinking about you, and missing you,' he explained without attempting to apologise. 'I knew I wouldn't sleep until I heard your voice.'

'Oh, Carl!' she laughed a little unsteadily, blinking back the tears that leapt into her eyes.

'Are you missing me?'

'Yes.'

The line crackled with silence for a moment, then he said distinctly, 'I wish you were here.'

Her heart was beating so hard and fast that she could hardly breathe. 'Are you telephoning from Washington?'

'Yes.'

'How long are you still going to be there?' she asked, determined to keep the conversation at an impersonal level.

'I shall have to stay on another day or two, then I leave for Wyoming.'

The line cleared slightly while he spoke, and she heard something in his voice that perturbed her. 'You sound tired.'

'I am,' he confessed, and before she could think of anything to say he groaned, 'God, Morgan, I wish I could hold you in my arms this very minute!' Her pulse rate quickened and her cheeks were flushed as she stood there speechless with a mixture of excitement and longing. 'Aren't you going to say something to that?' he demanded, with a hint of derisive laughter in his voice.

'Do they have a shortage of unattached females in America?' she questioned, forcing herself to sound flippant.

'There's no shortage, honey, only none of them have your delectable shape and size,' he quipped back.

'You flatter me!'

'Morgan,' he grunted from a long way away. 'When are you going to stop thinking of me as the big bad wolf?'

'When you can prove to me that you're not,' she replied without hesitation.

'If that's a challenge, than I accept it.'

'It wasn't a challenge,' she assured him hastily. 'I was being serious.'

'I was serious too, Morgan. Very serious.'

His voice came low and vibrant across the line, and when her senses responded to it she desperately tried to change the subject once more. 'This telephone call must be costing you the earth!'

'It's worth every cent just to hear your voice.'

'You're crazy!'

'Yes, honey,' he agreed. 'I'm crazy for you, if only you'll realise it.'

'Don't say things like that,' she rebuked him shakily.

'It's the truth,' he insisted roughly. 'If I could span the miles separating us then I would be there with you this minute, and holding you in my arms instead of lying here burning up inside with longing for you.'

Her own longing became a living, throbbing thing between them, binding them together across the vast distance that separated them physically, but she was still wary to accept without reserve what her heart craved most.

'Can I believe that you miss me that much?' she heard herself asking a little breathlessly.

'You can believe it,' he said simply and decisively.

'Carl . . .' She paused, too choked, and too incredibly happy to speak for a moment and, when she did, the words came straight from her heart. 'Don't stay away too long.'

'I'll be there as soon as I can make it, sweetheart.'

Did she imagine it, or was there a certain warmth in his voice which she had never heard before?

They said goodbye, and when the telephone link was severed between them Morgan buried her face in her shaking hands. 'Don't do this to me, Carl, unless you really mean it,' she moaned into her palms. 'Don't make me hope when there's nothing to hope for.'

Morgan could not go back to sleep after that. She made herself a cup of coffee and wondered time and again whether she had not given away too much of her feelings. She would have to be more careful in future. Carl was weaving his web of silk about her with expert precision, and although she was caught there was still a slight chance of escaping before she made a total prisoner of herself.

She felt exhausted by the time she arrived at the office that morning and, to make matters worse, Richard Kelly kept her in his office for almost two hours to take down dictation. On any other morning she would have welcomed it, but on that particular morning she was finding it difficult enough to concentrate with Richard rushing through some of the letters as if the devil was on his tail, and she sighed inwardly with relief when he finally leaned back in his chair, an indication that the session had come to an end.

'We were right about Gloria De La Rey,' he stopped her when she had almost reached the door. 'She *is* shielding someone.'

'A man?' Morgan questioned without much surprise, and her employer nodded grimly.

'He's at the head of a firm which is negotiating with her husband's organisation at the moment, and she's afraid that if her husband found out before the contract is signed he might ruin this chap's business.'

'Would he really do that?' she frowned.

'She would know her husband better than anyone else,' Richard reminded her. 'He's not too happy about divorcing her, you see, but at the moment Gloria is using his adultery as a leverage.'

'And if he found out about her boy-friend it might be stalemate?' she added almost thoughtfully.

'Exactly.'

'What happens now?'

'The divorce proceedings go ahead, of course,' Richard replied almost as if her question surprised him.

'Shouldn't her husband be allowed a second chance, considering that this was his first offence?' she wanted to know. 'I mean . . . marriage isn't something one enters into lightly, and there might still be something to salvage in their relationship.'

'My dear Morgan, I'm an attorney, not a marriage counsellor,' he laughed scornfully. 'If Gloria De La Rey wants a divorce, and she's adamant about it, then she's going to get it.'

'You don't really care, do you?' she accused, seeing for the first time a side of him that she did not like.

'It's not my job to care,' he explained tolerantly. 'Gloria De La Rey has grounds for a divorce, and so has her husband, but *she* is my client, and I don't intend to spill the beans, so to speak. If her husband somehow finds out about her boy-friend, and if it's not too late, then he may launch a counter-attack to stop the entire proceedings, but until then I'm going ahead with what information I have.'

It was logical, Morgan supposed, but she didn't like it, and, turning towards the door, she said coldly, 'I'd better get back to my desk and type these letters.'

She hammered away at the typewriter for the next hour, and only when a movement caught her eye did she look up from her work to find Richard Kelly leaning against the door jamb with a quizzical look on his rugged face.

'You're annoyed with me, aren't you.'

It was a statement, not a question, and it took the proverbial wind out of her sails. She stared at him for a moment, unable to think of anything to say, then she shrugged helplessly and smiled.

'It's your job, as you said, to do as your clients request, and just as long as it's within the confines of the law,' she acknowledged grudgingly. 'It's just as well that I'm not an attorney, because I'd end up caring too much for all the parties concerned, and that wouldn't put the butter on my bread!'

His grey eyes lit up, crinkling at the corners as he smiled. 'I'm relieved to know that you see it that way. I was beginning to think that my loyal secretary suddenly disliked me.'

'I was thinking with my heart instead of my head. 'I'm sorry,' she apologised lamely.

'You're forgiven,' he assured her, and Morgan felt the tension ease out of her after that.

She had been silly to let his statement anger her, and she was annoyed with herself for displaying so little understanding for a man who has always given only of his best to his clients.

Morgan was kept busy during the rest of that week, and she was grateful for it. It gave her less time to think of Carl, but the weekend followed its usual agonisingly slow pattern.

On the Thursday of the week thereafter she arrived home to find a letter from Carl in her postbox, and her heart seemed to do a double somersault in her breast as she clutched the letter against her and hurried towards the lift that would take her up to the seventh floor. She was anxious to read his letter, but also afraid; so afraid that, when she reached her flat, she put the letter on the low coffee table in the lounge, and left it there while she made herself a cup of coffee.

Her heart was bouncing wildly against her ribs, and her fingers were shaking when she finally slid her thumb nail beneath the flap and ripped open the envelope. She extracted a single sheet of thin air mail paper and, taking a deep breath, she unfolded it and started to read what he had written in his bold, masculine handwriting.

Morgan honey. She could almost hear his deep, velvety voice as she read those words. *I've been away from you before, but this time it's really got me where it hurts most. I find myself thinking so much about you that I can't concentrate on what I have to do, and I can't sleep nights without dreaming of you. You're with me in everything I say and do, and God only knows what you've done to me, because I think I'm going slowly crazy.*

Morgan lowered the letter on to her lap and closed her eyes. Stay calm, she warned her pounding heart. Could she believe what he had written, or was she reading something between the lines which was not there? Was she so hungry for some indication that he cared that she would accept simply anything as a budding declaration of love? Hot tears stung her eyelids and brought a lump to her throat, but she controlled herself with an effort, and tried to read the rest of his letter objectively.

I met my father in Washington one evening, and we had a long talk. I think there's a possibility that we should get along a little better in future, but I'll tell you all about it when I see you again.

They could only have discussed his mother, Morgan decided, and she could only hope that their discussion had led to a better understanding between them.

Tammy and the boys will be coming to the ranch for a few days next week, and I'm hoping it will ease the loneliness and the longing.

I miss you, Morgan. The ranch has always been like a little bit of paradise to me, but paradise has become hell this time around, and if there wasn't so much to do I'd leave here tomorrow.

She was doing it again, Morgan rebuked herself. She was reading too much into what he had written. With Carl it was a clear case of something out of reach seeming to be more attractive than something which was easily obtainable, and she had to cling to that thought for her own peace of mind.

Think of me kindly, sweet lady, he ended his letter, *and don't forget me while I'm gone. Yours, Carl.*

Her vision blurred, and the bold handwriting became distorted before her eyes. She would have been the happiest woman on earth if she could have taken his letter at face value, but she dared not. She had to remember that what he had to offer had nothing to do with love, and the usual commitments that went with it. What Carl wanted was an affair with no strings attached. It would last only until his interest waned, and that was the complete opposite of what she wanted where he was concerned.

She dashed away her ridiculous tears and read his letter through once again. When she came to the end she could not help but admire him for that touch of sincerity he had managed to weave into it, but then Carl was very clever, and *very* experienced in this sort of thing. He knew women like a harpist knew the strings of his instrument, and he knew exactly which strings to pluck for the desired effect. Carl had always succeeded in the past, and she supposed that he imagined he would eventually succeed with her. But not this time, she vowed silently, and not with me. He possessed her heart, and if that meant nothing to him then that was all that he would ever possess.

She folded the letter and slipped it back into the envelope. She was not going to be fooled by what he had written, but there was nothing she could do about that little voice in her heart that cried out in despair, 'But I *want* to believe what he implied in his letter!'

Morgan could not face another weekend alone in
Pretoria. She was awake before dawn on the Saturday
morning and, on the spur of the moment, she packed a
small suitcase, and decided to drive up to Rossmere.
The sun was barely rising when she left Pretoria
behind her, and if nothing unforeseen happened she
judged that she would arrive home in time to have
breakfast with her father. There was little traffic at
that time of the morning on the Great North Road,
and when she had passed the granite quarries at
Bon Accord she switched on her car radio. She
enjoyed travelling to the accompaniment of music,
and it always made the two-hour journey seem so much
shorter.

Rossmere had once been a mining town, but the
industrialists arrived after the luckless miners had left
their diggings, and factories had risen almost overnight
like mushrooms. That era had ended as well, and the
factories had made way for office buildings and shopping centres which still stood today. Rossmere had
been no more than an average size town, but Randolph
Hillier had considered it the ideal place to begin his
computer company, and he had expanded it into one
of the most important computer centres in the
country.

Morgan did not want to think of the Triton
Company. Thoughts of the Triton inevitably led to
Carl and, as it was, she had thought about him too
often since receiving his letter two days ago. She concentrated on her driving, and with the help of the radio
she somehow managed to channel her thoughts into a
different direction entirely for the duration of her
journey.

This was the first weekend she would be spending
at home since her return to Pretoria to have her
cast removed and, when she eventually drove
through the pillared entrance at the bottom end of
the driveway, she wondered nervously whether it had
been such a good idea to come home after all. This
was where she had met Carl, and the memory of the
impact he had made upon her at their first meeting
was something which would remain with her for
always.

Andrew Field came out on to the terrace when he
heard her car, and the happy smile on his angular
face was enough to disperse with her doubts.

'I was't expecting you home this weekend,' he said,
taking her suitcase from her and draping an arm
about her shoulders as he kissed her on the cheek.

'I only decided to come at the last minute,' she
explained as they went into the house. 'I simply
couldn't face this weekend on my own in the flat.'

Her father, fortunately, did not question her
statement, and Paulina's dark face brightened
with a toothy smile when she was instructed to
serve breakfast for two out on the side terrace.

There was plenty of news to catch up on; news of
old friends and family, but Andrew typically
refrained from talking about his work, and on
this occasion Morgan was grateful for it. She
talked instead about her own work, and about
some of the amusing incidents which had occurred
during recent weeks to brighten her own as well
as Richard Kelly's often painfully serious lives.
She told her father about Gloria De La Rey, knowing that he would keep this information to him-

self, and they laughed a little about Richard
Kelly's initial hesitance to see this woman alone
at his home.

As the day progressed, however, Morgan found
less to talk about, and long silences prevailed
which were unerringly filled with thoughts of
Carl. What was he doing? Was his sister still
visiting on the ranch with her children, or had
they returned to Washington? *Dammit*, she did not
want to think about him, but he stormed into her
thoughts during every unguarded moment, and it took
a tremendous effort of will to thrust him out again. It
was a lovely warm October day, and she did not want
to spoil it with unhappy thoughts, but she was not
entirely successful.

After dinner that evening, when she sat out on the
cool terrace with her father, he broke one of those long
silences by saying, 'Whatever it is that's on your mind,
Morgan, if you'd like to talk about it, then you're welcome to do so.'

Her father's perceptiveness startled her, and for a
moment she did not quite know what to do. She felt as
if she were being torn in two, and it was with a great
deal of uncertainty that she finally said: 'I'd like to talk
about it, but I don't think you're going to be happy
with what I have to say.'

His chair creaked beneath him in the moonlit darkness, and he lit one of those long cigars he occasionally
smoked. 'If it will ease your mind to talk, then I'm
prepared to listen open-mindedly.'

Morgan clasped and unclasped her hands nervously
in her lap. 'I think——' she began, then she paused
and shook her head. 'No, it's gone beyond that. I *know*

I'm in love with Carl. I tried very hard not to love him, but I—I couldn't help myself.'

The pungent aroma of Andrew's cigar made her nostrils quiver, and she suddenly found herself fighting desperately against the ridiculous desire to laugh and cry simultaneously. Hearing her own voice confessing her feelings for Carl had sounded like something close to a death sentence, and during the strained silence that followed she wondered how her father was taking it.

'How does Carl feel about you?' he finally asked, and she felt his eyes observing her intently in the darkness.

'I know he wants me,' the words were torn from her, then she gestured helplessly with her hands. 'Oh, Dad, I don't know what to do!'

'Are you considering having an affair with him?'

His question shook her, making her recall one particular occasion when she had been terribly tempted to cast aside her rigid principles, but she kept this to herself and said quietly, 'If I had an affair with him, then I would be acting against everything I've always held most sacred.'

An agitated gust of cigar smoke drifted her way. 'What are you hoping for, then?'

'I'm not sure,' she sighed, getting up from her chair and crossing the terrace to lean against one of the tall, concrete pillars. The stars glittered brightly in the night sky, and crickets chirped in the shrubs below the terrace, but she neither heard nor saw anything at that moment. 'I received a letter from Carl on Thursday, and he wrote certain things in it that made me think he might care for me in a special way, but——' She paused abruptly and, swinging round to face her father, she asked with a note of anguish in her voice, 'How will I know if he's absolutely sincere? How can I ever be sure that I can trust him?'

Andrew was silent for a moment, his cigar forgotten between his fingers while he pondered her question, then he said philosophically, 'In every situation, or relationship, there's a crucial point that must be reached, and when you're there you'll know whether he's sincere, and whether you can trust him.'

'Oh, lord,' she laughed unsteadily a moment later. 'This is all speculation to which I've added a large slice of wishful thinking, really. Carl told me himself that he wasn't the marrying kind, and I can't see a future in any other kind of relationship.'

'Forgive me for saying this,' her father said darkly, 'but I did warn you.'

'I know,' Morgan swallowed convulsively. 'I thought I could cope. I found his advances amusing at first, and I mocked him because of it, but my strategy didn't work. I no longer find it funny, and I wish to heaven I could.'

'When the heart is involved it becomes a deadly serious game.'

'And a painful one.' she added bitterly, returning to her chair and hovering on the brink of tears.

'I wish I could help you,' Andrew said sympathetically.

Morgan admired her father very much at that moment. He had warned her against Carl, and he had never liked the idea that she was seeing him, and yet he was still willing to help if he could. The tears were very close, but she pulled herself together fiercely, and changed the subject.

'Are there still rumours that the Triton may become a subsidiary company to Carl's firm in America?'

'The rumours are still rife,' Andrew admitted, 'but Carl has called for a board meeting during the first week in November, and I have a feeling that we'll all know exactly where we stand afterwards.'

She digested this in silence for a moment. 'I wonder how Randolph Hillier will feel about this.'

'When Hillier retired he stressed the fact that he was leaving all future decisions in Carl's capable hands. Hillier is, of course, still the founder-director, and as such a member of the board, but when he retired he denounced his right to vote on any business level.'

'In other words, he's welcome to attend the board meetings, and to enter into the discussions, but if something were to be put to the vote he would have to step aside?'

'That's it,' Andrew confirmed, puffing at his cigar and sending a cloud of aromatic smoke her way.

'He could influence the decision of the other members, though,' she remarked thoughtfully.

'He could, but I doubt if he would stand in the way of progress,' her father pointed out. 'With Carl's firm in the U.S.A. behind the Triton, there's only one way the company could go, and that's up.'

Morgan felt a little stunned. 'Carl's computer firm is an influential one, then?'

'One of *the* biggest and most influential in the States,' Andrew confirmed, brushing ash off his trousers. 'I'll say this for Carl Ziegler, he works hard, and seldom spares himself. He's usually the first to arrive at the office in the morning, and the last to leave at night. He sets high standards for himself, and he seldom tolerates anything less from his staff.'

'He'll burn himself out if he's not careful,' she commented to no one in particular.

'Tell *him* that, not me,' Andrew laughed.

'I have told him, but there's no reason why he should take my advice.' She glanced at her father speculatively. 'Would it put less strain on him if the Triton became a subsidiary company?'

'It would put considerably less strain on him, yes,' her father agreed. 'All he would need would be someone with sufficient knowledge and authority who could hold the Triton reins firmly.'

'Is there such a man?'

'There are several.'

'Could you?' she asked curiously.

'I could, but I see no reason why Carl should consider me more capable than any of the others,' Andrew replied modestly. 'I'm not so sure that I really want that kind of responsibility at my age.'

'It would be a challenge,' she pointed out.

'Who needs a challenge when they're seven years away from the retirement age?' he laughed scoffingly.

'You're not decrepit,' she almost scolded him.

'Listen, my girl,' he said, leaning forward and patting her arm. 'We're speculating again, and that could be dangerous.'

'I think I'll go to bed,' she said eventually, stifling a yawn behind her hand as she got to her feet. 'I want to leave after breakfast in the morning.'

Andrew's face mirrored his disappointment. 'I thought you were going to spend the day here tomorrow as well.'

'What about your Sunday golf championship?' she

questioned with a suggestion of a smile hovering about her mouth.

'You could always come with me,' he suggested.

'Daddy, I love you,' she laughed, 'but not to the extent where I would enjoy traipsing around after you on a seemingly endless course in the hot sun.'

'So your love has limits?' he teased.

'Very definite limits,' she quipped back, dropping a light kiss on his forehead. 'Goodnight, Dad.'

Morgan lay in bed that night and once again her thoughts revolved around Carl, but this time she realised something which she had missed before. Her father had seldom paid much attention to rumours, so there had to be some truth in the rumour concerning the Triton's merger with Carl's company in the States, and if Carl was thinking of returning permanently to the U.S.A., then where, *exactly*, did that leave her?

Nothing made sense, and the more she thought about it, the more baffled she became. If she could believe what Carl had written in his letter, then what did he have in mind for her when he left South Africa? Or must she interpret his letter as a last desperate attempt to persuade her into a brief affair with him before he walked out of her life permanently?

It made painful sense, she had to admit it, but deep down in her heart she could not wholly accept it, and that tiny flicker of hope refused to be doused entirely.

CHAPTER EIGHT

MORGAN returned home from work one afternoon during the following week, and sensed that she was not alone in her flat even before she saw the superbly built man who uncoiled his great length from its reclining position on the sofa. He had unknotted his tie, and his shirt had been unbuttoned almost to his waist to reveal the tight curls of golden body hair against his tanned chest. Her hands suddenly ached to touch him, and her heart seemed to be beating in her throat.

'Carl!' she breathed his name, meeting the onslaught of those lazy eyes observing her with a faint smile in their blue depths. 'How—How did you get in?'

'The caretaker very kindly let me in with his skeleton key after he'd checked out my credentials with your father.' His mouth curved into that mocking smile she remembered so well as he lessened the distance between them. 'Do you mind?'

'Of course I don't mind,' she whispered hoarsely, her eyes sliding hungrily over the length and breadth of him. 'I wasn't expecting you, that's all.'

Morgan fought desperately against the wild longing to fling herself into his arms, but his nearness stunted her reasoning, and she swayed towards him. She was caught at once and crushed against the hard length of him in a fierce embrace, and when he set his mouth on hers she felt as if she were drowning helplessly in the wave of emotions that swept over her. She clung to

him, her hands moving hungrily over shoulders that
seemed too wide to accommodate the white silk shirt,
and she felt the muscles rippling beneath her fingers as
his arms tightened about her almost convulsively. He
kissed her again and again; long drugging kisses that
seemed to draw her very soul through her parted,
eager lips, and when at last he eased his mouth from
hers she felt drained and weak.

'Do you know how I feel at this moment?' he
asked while his eyes devoured her, and she shook her
head, her heart too full to speak. 'I feel as though I
just want to hold you in my arms like this, and never
let you go.'

His mouth descended to capture hers this time with
a sensual hunger that seared through her, and robbed
her of the desire to resist when his hands roamed her
body as if to reacquaint themselves with every contour.
It was a long time before he finally released her and,
when he did, she found she was shaking with the longing to fling herself back into his arms, but with a tremendous effort she managed to control herself.

'I expected to see you looking refreshed after your
sojourn on the ranch,' she said with remarkable calmness when she noticed at last the lines of tiredness
beneath his eyes and along the sides of his mouth.

'It wasn't exactly all pleasure, honey. There was a
lot to do on the ranch, and I was also in daily contact
with the office in Washington.' Carl pushed his fingers
through his hair and it feel back untidily across his
broad forehead. 'I was in the thick of a very important
negotiation, and it was something I couldn't leave in
the hands of my second in command.'

Did these important negotiations have anything to

do with the Triton? she wondered as she said hopefully, 'Want to tell me about it?'

'Some other time,' he sighed, taking her hand and drawing her towards the sofa. 'Did you get my letter?'

'Yes,' she said as he pulled her down beside him, but she shied away nervously from its personal contents. 'Tell me about your father.'

His eyes mocked her momentarily as if he had sensed her thoughts, then his expression sobered. 'You were right, you know, about there being two sides to every story. My father was reluctant to discuss the subject and remained oddly loyal to the memory of my mother, but I somehow gathered that their marriage had lost its spark long before he'd stepped over the line to seek female company elsewhere. We talked a long time, but I didn't get much more out of him. I finally called on a woman who used to be a very close friend of my mother's, and she told me everything I wanted to know. It appears my parents discovered soon after Tammy's birth that their marriage had been a mistake, but for our sakes they remained together, and they were happy in a sense even though their marriage wasn't fulfilling in every respect. My mother knew about my father's affairs, but they'd both forfeited the right to object about what the other did, and . . . well, that's the story as I know it now.'

'I'm sorry,' Morgan whispered, staring down at the large hand clasping hers, and marvelling at the fine white hair on the back of it which contrasted so heavily with his tanned skin. 'The truth isn't always pleasant.'

'Knowing the truth has made me realise once again how dicy marriage is if you're not absolutely sure it's what you want,' Carl told her roughly, then he raised her hand to his lips and she felt their warmth against her knuckles. 'Did you miss me?'

The truth leapt into the grey-green eyes which were raised to his, and she had no option but to confirm it with a husky, 'Yes, I missed you.'

He raised a hand and tugged the pins from her hair before she could stop him, and it fell in thick silken waves on to her shoulders. 'Did you miss me enough to——'

'No,' she interrupted him abruptly, steeling herself against the pleasurable sensations aroused by those clever fingers caressing the nape of her neck. 'I haven't changed my mind about going to bed with you.'

'You really are a tough nut to crack, aren't you?' he laughed softly, trailing tantalising fingers along her throat and down to the V of her blouse.

'Would you like a cup of coffee?' she changed the subject, moving beyond his reach before his fingers could explore the hollow between her breasts.

'Yes, and then I must be on my way.' Carl stretched out his long legs and laced his fingers behind his fair head. 'I could do with a good night's sleep before I return to the office tomorrow.'

'Did you fly in this morning?' Morgan asked as she got to her feet.

'Yes, but I stayed on in Johannesburg until quite late this afternoon.' He saw the flicker of suspicion in her eyes before she could veil it, and his mouth twisted derisively. 'It was business, not pleasure.'

'I'll make the coffee,' she said tersely, turning from him abruptly to hide the flush that surged up into her cheeks.

She stood there in the kitchen waiting for the water

to boil in the kettle, and realised the helplessness of the situation. There would always be that little spark of suspicion and doubt to mar their relationship, and it would prevent her from trusting him as implicitly as she would wish to. With no written, or verbal commitment to bind him, he would be free to walk out on her whenever it pleased him, and what would be the sense in leaping into a relationship with a man who was planning on leaving the country soon. If the rumours concerning the future of the Triton were true, then she doubted very much whether he would stay on in South Africa, and she was not so sure that she would accompany him to the States . . . *if* he asked her to.

Morgan berated herself mentally. She was indulging in wishful thinking again, and that was a futile occupation. There was no reason at all why Carl would ask her to accompany him to the States and, even if he did, she would not go with him; not under the circumstances which she knew he preferred.

When Carl left half an hour later she felt restless and disturbed. She tried to read, but that didn't help, and neither did she manage to relax while listening to her favourite records. She finally went to bed and, surprisingly, slept away the hours until morning.

Morgan was taking a welcome break with a cup of tea on the Friday afternoon of that same week when she looked up to see Richard Kelly approaching her desk.

'I have a rather difficult brief here that I'd like to work on over the weekend,' he explained, handing her a file which contained his handwritten notes. 'Do you think you could stay on a bit later this evening to type these notes for me?'

'If you won't mind giving me a lift home afterwards,' she smiled up at him apologetically. 'My car is in for a repair job and I came to work on the bus this morning.'

Richard nodded and gave her one of those absent little smiles. 'It will be a pleasure to take you home.'

There was nothing unusual about staying late at the office to type out his notes on a certain brief, she had done it often enough in the past, and she was quite happy to do so on that particular evening until the telephone on her desk rang a few minutes later. She lifted the receiver to her ear and held it there with her shoulder while she fed a clean sheet of paper into the typewriter.

'Mr Kelly's office, good afternoon,' she said into the mouthpiece.

'Hi, Morgan.' Her hands stilled on the machine at the sound of Carl's voice. 'I'm coming to Pretoria late this afternoon, and I'll be staying at the same hotel as always. What about meeting me there after work for a quiet drink and dinner?'

'I'm afraid I can't, Carl,' she declined regretfully. 'I'll be working late this evening, and I have no idea what time I'll be finished.'

'I'll give you until seven-thirty,' he said amiably. 'If you're not there by that time then I'll have dinner and treat myself to an early night for a change.'

'I'll try my best, but I can't promise anything.'

'That's good enough for me,' he replied hurriedly. 'See you, honey, and if it's not this evening, then it will be tomorrow some time.'

Morgan replaced the receiver moments later and allowed herself the luxury of nursing her disappointment for a few minutes before she settled down to work once more.

She worked on steadily during the remainder of the afternoon and into the early evening, pausing only briefly when Richard came in with a further batch of handwritten notes. When she finally pulled the last sheet of paper from the typewriter she glanced at the clock against the wall and was surprised to see that it was a quarter to seven. Her heart lifted, there was still time to meet Carl for dinner, and her hands were almost shaking with excitement when she cleared her desk and handed Richard the file of typed notes.

'Do you think you could drop me off at a hotel in the city?' she asked when she sat beside him in his Mercedes.

'Certainly,' he smiled at her, and when she gave him the name of the hotel he asked, 'Are you meeting someone there?'

'Yes, a—a friend,' she stammered a little foolishly, and she was angry with herself for blushing like a schoolgirl.

Richard drove on in silence; a silence which he broke a few minutes later by saying casually. 'There's the hotel you want, straight up ahead.'

Morgan nodded without speaking, her heart bouncing in her chest, and when he parked his car a little distance from the entrance, she put her hand out rather blindly towards the handle and said gratefully, 'Thank you very much, I really do appreciate your coming out of your way, and I——'

She paused abruptly, the words stilling in her throat, and an icy coldness spreading through her body when she saw two people emerge from the entrance of the hotel. It was Carl, and his fair head was lowered towards a beautiful, dark-haired young woman who was leaning rather heavily on his arm. Morgan recognised the woman as well; it was Gloria De La Rey, and they were both so absorbed in each other that neither of them noticed the two people staring at them from within the Mercedes. They got into Carl's silver Porsche and drove away at speed, and only then did Richard notice the white, shaken expression on Morgan's face, and the tortured look in her eyes as they followed the Porsche until it disappeared from sight.

'Is something wrong, Morgan? Are you feeling ill?' he asked, leaning towards her anxiously.

She swallowed convulsively, but that tightness in her throat remained immovable. 'I'm fine, I—I——'

He studied her closely when she faltered to a stop, and asked shrewdly, 'Was that the chap you came here to meet?'

'Yes,' she croaked, feeling as though the earth's solid foundations had dropped out beneath her, and her insides seemed to have difficulty in righting themselves after the severe jolt it had received.

Carl had wasted no time in finding someone else when he had thought that she might not make it, and of all people his choice had to fall on Gloria De La Rey, Morgan thought bitterly.

'It seems he got tired of waiting,' Richard jabbed a cruel finger into an open wound, 'but now we know the identity of the other man in my client's life.'

Morgan had not given the latter a thought until that moment, and although a part of her rejected the idea, it somehow seemed as though the last pieces of the puzzle were falling into place. Carl was a businessman. It was possible that he could be negotiating some sort of deal with Gloria's husband, and it was possible—it hurt to think about it, but she had to—it *was* possible that Carl had been using her to cover up his relationship with Gloria De La Rey.

'But what about that letter he wrote to you from America?' her heart questioned.

'That was intended to pull the wool more securely over your eyes,' her mind replied bitterly.

Oh, God, but he was *despicable*!

'What about having a plate of soup and a sandwich somewhere with me?' Richard interrupted her thoughts.

Morgan drew a painful breath. 'That's very kind of you, but I——'

'I'm not taking "no" for an answer,' he cut in adamantly, and she felt too mentally exhausted to argue.

'Thank you,' she nodded listlessly. 'I accept your invitation.'

Richard took her to a cosy little diner in the city which was not too crowded, but she felt she could not face the chicken sandwiches after she had forced herself to swallow down a plate of tasty vegetable soup. Richard insisted, however, and she somehow managed to satisfy him by eating one sandwich. When they finally lingered over their coffee she felt that cold, numb feeling slipping slowly away from her, and it was replaced by a warmth that stole through her body.

'Would it help at all to talk about it?' Richard asked eventually.

'Not really,' she shook her head, that haunted look still very much in her eyes.

'Does he live here in Pretoria?' Richard continued to question her in a manner true to his profession.

'He's from Rossmere,' she replied, not elaborating further.

'So he's here for the weekend?'

'I presume so.'

'He asked you to meet him at the hotel this evening?'

She looked up into those grey eyes observing her so intently, and afraid of what he might be thinking, she explained hastily, 'He invited me to have dinner with him, and when I told him I would be working late he gave me until seven-thirty to get there.'

'And it's only seven-thirty now,' Richard remarked, glancing at his watch.

'Yes,' she whispered, lowering her glance to the untouched cup of coffee in front of her, and wishing suddenly that she were dead.

'He'll have a lot of explaining to do when you see him tomorrow,' Richard observed drily, and an unexpected wave of anger surged through her.

'I don't want to see him again,' she snapped fiercely. 'I don't *ever* want to see him again!'

Hot tears stung the back of her eyelids, but she blinked them away rapidly. She was not going to waste her tears on someone as undeserving as Carl. He had almost succeeded in making her believe that he cared, but she saw him for what he was; a man who had used her shamelessly as a cover-up for his affair with a married woman. It was disgusting and degrading, and she could never forgive him for doing this to her.

Richard drove her home a little while later, and when they arrived at her flat she turned to him and said politely, 'Thank you very much for being so kind, Mr Kelly.'

'It was a pleasure,' he assured her hastily, 'and don't you think we've known each other long enough for you to call me Richard?'

'I—I couldn't!' She stared at him in surprise. 'You're my employer!'

'Then I'm making it an order,' he announced without smiling. 'From now on you call me Richard. Do I make myself clear?'

She hesitated, not quite knowing what to say at first, then she nodded and said: 'Perfectly clear ... Richard.'

A brief smile touched his lips, then he sobered once again and said abruptly, 'Goodnight, Morgan.'

She remained where she was until the lift doors had closed behind him, then she went into her flat and locked the door behind her. Richard Kelly had been very kind and considerate. He had helped her through those first painfully awkward moments, and she would always be thankful for that.

Morgan felt strangely calm as she bathed and went to bed. It felt as if her heart had been wrenched out of her chest to leave her with no feeling at all, but when she switched off her bedside light her calmness suddenly deserted her, and she cried herself to sleep.

Her tears did nothing to ease the situation, it simply made her feel heavy-eyed and exhausted the following morning. She went out early to collect her Mini at the garage, and to do her shopping for the weekend. When she returned to her flat two hours later the telephone was ringing, but she did not answer it. She sensed that it would be Carl, and he was the last person on earth she wanted to talk to at that moment. She still felt too raw inside, and too angry. She had had no business falling in love with him, and now she was reaping the results of her foolish behaviour, but *this* was where it would all end!

The telephone continued to ring and, when it finally stopped, a new fear took possession of her. What would she do if Carl came to the flat? She bit her lip nervously, and, making a snap decision, she hurried out of her flat and took the lift down to the caretaker's flat on the ground floor.

'Mr Olivier,' she began almost breathlessly when the elderly, robust-looking man opened his door. 'I wonder if I could ask you to do me a favour?'

'Why, certainly, Miss Field,' he assured her at once in his usual friendly manner.

Morgan hesitated only briefly, then the words came out in a rush. 'If a Mr Carl Ziegler should question you about my whereabouts some time during today or tomorrow, would you tell him that I've gone away for the weekend with friends?'

'You don't want to see him, is that it?' he questioned with a swift understanding that surprised her.

'Exactly,' she confirmed truthfully.

'I'll give him that message,' Mr Olivier promised, and she sighed inwardly with relief.

'Thank you so much,' she breathed, then she took the lift up to the seventh floor again, and closeted herself in her flat.

The telephone rang several times that morning, but she did not risk answering it. If she spoke to Carl now she would burst into tears, and that was the last thing she wanted to do.

Her doorbell rang shortly after two that afternoon, and the sound jarred her nerves. Her hands clutched the arms of her chair so tightly that her knuckles showed white through the skin, but she sat there, not daring to move. The doorbell rang again, impatiently this time, and although everything within her suddenly cried out for her to open the door, she bit down hard on her lip, and remained seated. She did not want to see Carl, and she did not want to speak to him. He would have a glib answer ready if she should question him about last night; men like him were always clever at wriggling out of a difficult situation, but she was tired of being made a fool of. She had known what kind of man he was right from the start, but, like a gullible fool, she had come close to letting him convince her that he was serious; that she was someone special to him, and that had been her biggest mistake. Her father had warned her, every instinct within her mind and heart had warned her, but she had ignored all those warnings, and had gone ahead until her heart had become hopelessly involved.

Her doorbell did not ring again, and some minutes later the caretaker slipped a note under her door to tell her that he had passed on her message to Carl. Her hands shook and her eyes blurred with tears as she found herself facing the agonising truth. She could avoid seeing Carl, but she could never avoid the pain of loving him. He had lied to her, and he had used her in the most despicable way, but she would love him until the day she died.

She curled herself up on the sofa and wept unrestrainedly, the choking sobs tearing at her insides, and she did not stop until, drained and exhausted, she drifted into a deep sleep from which she awoke several hours later. Her limbs were stiff and cramped when she got to her feet, and her eyelids felt swollen and heavy. She washed her face and brushed her hair, then she tried to eat something, but nothing would go down, and she finally settled for a cup of strong coffee to revive her. *To the devil with Carl*! she remonstrated with herself eventually. She had got along without him before, and she would get along without him again. It might take a little time to adjust herself, but she would succeed in the end.

Morgan spent the rest of the weekend with the telephone unplugged at the wall, and on the Monday morning, when Richard Kelly was half way through his dictation, he looked up abruptly to say, 'I wanted to phone and find out how you were, but I had a feeling that you wouldn't be taking any calls.'

'I unplugged the telephone,' she confessed guiltily.

'I thought so,' he murmured, observing her intently. 'Did he try to contact you again?'

'He came to the flat on Saturday afternoon, and I knew that he would eventually make enquiries about me when there was no answer, so I took the precaution of asking the caretaker to tell him that I was away for the weekend.'

'Are you serious about not wanting to see him again?'

'Would you want to see a woman who had used you to cover up her affair with another man?' she counter-questioned tritely.

'You've made you point,' Richard replied in a tight-lipped manner, then he continued his dictation as if there had been no interruption at all.

Morgan's telephone at the flat rang incessantly on the Tuesday evening, and she was seriously thinking of unplugging it again when the thought crossed her mind that it might be her father trying to contact her. He often called to hear how she was, but she could not take that chance. She waited instead until it had stopped ringing, then she lifted the receiver quickly and dialled her father's number in Rossmere.

'Were you perhaps trying to get through to me, Daddy?' she asked when her father answered the telephone almost the very instant it started ringing.

'I was, but there's obviously something wrong with your telephone,' he replied exasperatedly, and she did not advise him to the contrary. 'Were you away this past weekend, Morgan?'

'I was,' she lied uncomfortably, and surprised that he should ask. 'Why do you want to know?'

'Carl seemed to be rather concerned about you,' Andrew explained. 'He told me he'd spoken to you on the telephone the Friday afternoon, and that you never said a word about going away, but after several unsuccessful attempts to contact you he found out that you'd gone to friends.'

Morgan felt herself stiffen. 'Did he ask you to ring me?'

'I sometimes worry about you too, you know,' said Andrew, and she suddenly felt ashamed of herself.

'I'm fine, Daddy,' she said eventually. 'There's nothing for you to worry about.'

'I'll pass that on to Carl as well.'

'You don't have to pass anything on to him,' she almost snapped.

Andrew Field was silent for a moment, then he asked

abruptly, 'Have you and Carl had an argument about something?'

'There's been no argument,' she said, choosing her words carefully, 'but I've finally realised what a fool I was to think I could trust him in any way.'

'You've reached that crucial point, then?' her father questioned, referring to the discussion they had had during her recent visit to her home.

'Yes, I have.'

'I see.' The line crackled with silence for a moment, then he said: 'I'm sorry, Morgan. I was afraid all along that you would be hurt, and now my fears have become a reality.'

'I've been hurt,' she said quickly, and with false bravado, 'but I'll get over it.'

'I sincerely hope so,' Andrew replied.

Morgan went to bed shortly after speaking to her father, but it was a long time before she went to sleep. She was not a baby, she told herself firmly. She was almost twenty-five, and she was not going to fall apart at the seams because one man had succeeded in making her heart beat a little faster. She loved him, but *so what*? She would learn to love again in time, and with any luck she would feel that way about someone who was more worthy of her love.

These thoughts sustained her during the week, but her composure slipped badly when the telephone on her desk rang the Friday afternoon and Carl's familiar 'Hi, honey' rang in her ears. The blood surged into her cheeks, then receded to leave her deathly pale, and it was at this point that Richard walked into her office.

'Hello, Carl,' she said in a deceptively calm voice, and at the same time she answered Richard's silent query.

'Why didn't you tell me when I spoke to you last Friday that you would be going away for the weekend?' Carl demanded without preamble.

'It slipped my mind,' she lied.

'Will I see you this evening?'

'This evening? Well, I . . .'

She felt trapped, then she looked up to see Richard gesturing and mouthing the words, 'You're having dinner with me this evening.'

'I'm afraid I can't see you this evening,' she told Carl while casting a grateful glance in Richard's direction. 'I've already accepted an invitation to dinner.'

'Will I see you tomorrow?'

'Tomorrow?' she echoed stupidly, and once again Richard threw out a lifeline which she grasped at desperately.

'You're spending the weekend with friends,' Richard mouthed the words in a whisper, jabbing his thumb into his chest.

'I—I'm sorry, Carl, but I'm spending the weekend with friends,' she repeated like a parrot copying its master.

'Dammit, Morgan, when am I going to see you?' Carl's voice exploded in her ear.

'I don't really know,' she replied evasively.

'What about next weekend?'

'I'm not quite sure about next weekend, but there's a possibility that I might be going away as well,' she lied, her heart beating so hard and fast during the ensuing silence that she was almost certain Carl could hear it.

'Are you giving me the brush-off, Morgan?' he demanded in a dangerously quiet voice.

'What on earth has given you that idea?' she asked with mock innocence.

'My instinct warns me that for some reason you're trying to avoid me, and I'm seldom wrong.'

'I can't neglect my friends simply because of you, Carl, and I'm sure you'll have no difficulty in finding someone else to spend your time with,' she told him coldly. 'Now you really must excuse me, but I have a pile of work on my desk that I have to wade through before I can go home this evening.'

She said an abrupt 'Goodbye', and only when she had to fumble the receiver on to its cradle did she realise how much she was shaking.

'About this evening . . .' she began when she had succeeded in gathering her scattered wits about her.

'You're having dinner with me, as I said,' Richard told her.

'I accept gladly, but the weekend . . .'

'I'm having a few friends over at my place,' he interrupted her, 'and I'd like you to join us.'

'But your friends might think that—that you and I——'

'That we're more than fond of each other?' he finished for her with a twisted little smile.

'Yes,' she nodded, her cheeks colouring with embarrassment.

'They're free to think what they like as far as I'm concerned.' he brushed the matter aside.

'Richard . . .' She hesitated, not wanting to hurt him, but she had to speak her mind. 'I accepted your invitation in theory, and it served its purpose. Carl won't be coming to Pretoria this weekend, at least not to see *me*, so there's no need to carry out your invitation in practice.'

'Lies have a way of surfacing when you least expect it,' he explained tolerantly. 'If you accept my invitation for the weekend then you haven't lied about it.'

She stared at him a little confusedly. 'I don't know why you should go to such lengths to help me in my personal life.'

'I was there when you saw him leaving the hotel with Gloria De La Rey, and I saw what it did to you,' he explained in a harsh voice that she had never heard him use before. 'I don't ever want to see you hurt that much again.'

He turned on his heel and disappeared into his office, leaving Morgan to stare after him in bewilderment. She would not mind so much if Richard Kelly simply felt sorry for her, but she sincerely hoped that he was not developing stronger feelings for her. She would hate to hurt him after all the kindness he had showered on her.

CHAPTER NINE

RICHARD KELLY had been Morgan's employer for almost four years, but when she faced him across the small table in the restaurant with its mirrored walls and concealed lighting, it felt to her as if she were dining with an old friend instead of the man who paid her salary every month, and she relaxed to the extent where she might have succeeded in shutting Carl out of her mind had Richard not mentioned his name.

'I have some news for you which I think might alter your feelings with regard to Carl Ziegler,' he announced while they were waiting for their coffee to be served. 'Gloria De La Rey telephoned me at my home earlier this evening and cancelled her application for a divorce.'

Morgan digested this in silence before she spoke. 'That doesn't alter my feelings at all. It simply means that she's finally discovered, like so many other women, that Carl has no intention of marrying her.'

'What makes you so sure that that's the reason?'

'What woman in her right mind would leave her husband for the insecurity of living with a man who might walk out on her tomorrow, or the day after?' she answered his question with one of her own, then she added derisively, 'Carl's not the marrying sort. He told me so himself.'

Richard's eyebrows rose sharply. 'Then why . . .?'

'Why did I let myself care for him?' she voiced the

question he seemed to be having difficulty in phrasing, and her mouth curved with the bitterness that welled up inside of her. 'It isn't easy dictating to one's heart. I knew what he was, I knew all the dangers involved, but for some inexplicable reason I found myself hoping for the impossible, and I was almost beginning to believe that I actually meant something to him when— when I saw him with Mrs De La Rey the other evening. I realised then that he'd been playing a double game, and now I despise him for it.'

'We haven't any proof that he *is* the man she was having an affair with,' Richard argued.

'Could you give me any other valid reason why they should have been together that evening?' Morgan demanded sarcastically, but she winced inwardly as she experienced again the pain and disillusionment she had felt that evening a week ago.

'What you have is nothing more than circumstantial evidence. He could have been with her for any number of reasons.'

'You're arguing like an attorney,' she accused with a mirthless laugh, 'and you're totally contradicting my statement the other day that you didn't care about people.'

'I *do* care, Morgan,' he assured her urgently, leaning towards her slightly, 'but in my job I have to deal with facts, and if you were the opposing counsel in this instance I would tell you quite bluntly that you haven't enough factual evidence to convict your man of the crime he's accused of.'

'Whose side are you on?' she demanded mockingly.

'Yours, naturally,' he replied drily, 'but I feel it's my duty to point out certain flaws in the foundations of your case. At first, when I saw my client with Carl Ziegler, I jumped to the natural conclusion that this was the secret man in her life, but I've been doing a great deal of thinking since then, and I realised that I had no proof at all in this matter. My investigations have led nowhere, and least of all in Carl Ziegler's direction.'

Morgan stared at him aghast. 'You've had Carl investigated?'

'I have,' came the abrupt reply, 'and I found absolutely nothing to connect him with my client in any way.'

Morgan experienced a twinge of doubt. Perhaps she had judged Carl too hastily, but that still left unexplained the reason why he should have had Gloria De La Rey hanging on his arm with such familiarity. Circumstantial evidence? Coincidence? Her heart fluttered hopefully, but her mind remained stoically unmoved. It was too much of a coincidence that Carl should have been with that particular woman that evening, and that made it all the more difficult for her to believe that there had been nothing to it.

Richard changed the subject after their coffee had been served, and told her briefly about his friends, Graham and Sandra Larkan, whom he was expecting from Johannesburg for the weekend.

'Graham and I studied Law together, and we've kept in touch ever since,' he explained. 'You'll like his wife, Sandra. They've only been married a little over two years, and they've been doing their level best during that time to encourage me into what they call "matrimonial bliss".'

'Have you never thought of getting married?' Morgan quizzed him tentatively.

'I've thought of it many times,' he grinned, 'but what's the use of thinking about it when the right woman hasn't come along to fill the vacancy?'

'I don't think you've actually taken the time to get to know many women. You're always shutting yourself away with a brief, and planning a defence, and you won't meet the right woman that way.'

'Are you suggesting that I should neglect my work in favour of leading a more social life?' Richard asked mockingly.

'There's a time to work, and a time to play,' she argued quietly, thinking momentarily of Carl who somehow succeeded in doing both so zealously.

'You think I don't set aside sufficient time for socialising with the opposite sex?' Richard broke into her thoughts, and she smiled at him apologetically.

'I don't think you can honestly say that you do.'

He did not reply to this, and her thoughts drifted irrevocably back to Carl. He was almost the exact opposite to Richard Kelly. A woman would never need to doubt Richard. He was perhaps a bit dull at times, but he was as dependable as a rock. Carl, on the other hand, was exciting to be with. He could charm you into a state where you actually believed you were something special, but he was reliable and dependable only where his work was concerned. Richard had given the impression that he would welcome marriage if he should meet the right woman, but Carl only welcomed the thought of a woman in his bed with no legal commitments.

Morgan groaned inwardly. She was being made increasingly aware of what a fool she had been to allow

herself to fall in love with a man who was the exact
antithesis of everything she had always hoped for in
the man of her choice. She could almost laugh at her
stupidity if it were not so tragic, but at that moment
she felt much closer to tears.

When Richard took her home that evening it was
arranged that she would be at his home at ten o'clock
the Saturday morning, and she was surprised to find
herself looking forward to the weekend which she had
viewed with such reluctance initially.

Morgan enjoyed the drive out to Richard's home the
following morning. The jacaranda trees were ablaze
with mauve blossoms that spilled on to the streets and
pavements like a flowery carpet, and Morgan loved
Pretoria at this time of the year when it lived up to its
name of the 'Jacaranda City'.

At ten o'clock sharp she parked her Mini in
Richard's driveway, and, when he came out to meet
her, she discovered that his friends had arrived a few
minutes earlier. She was ushered into the house, and
while her small suitcase was being taken to her room,
Morgan was introduced to Graham Larkan and his
wife Sandra. Graham was tall, lean, and severe-look-
ing, but his features were lightened by a hint of
humour in his eyes. His wife was small and fair with
an expressive, decidedly mischievous face, and Morgan
found herself liking them instantly.

The Larkans accepted Morgan's presence in
Richard's home with no outward sign of curiosity, but
that afternoon, when Morgan found herself alone with
Sandra beside the swimming pool, there was undis-
guised curiosity in the eyes of Graham Larkan's wife.

'Forgive me for asking, but ... are you and Richard ...?'

'No,' Morgan replied firmly when Sandra paused selfconsciously. 'I'm his secretary, I was at a loose end this weekend, and he simply invited me to make up a foursome.'

'Oh ... pity,' Sandra smiled mischievously. 'But I'm glad he invited you, or I might have found myself becoming bored with my own company while the men lose themselves in their usual discussions involving their profession!'

The conversation drifted on to safer ground, but Morgan found herself thinking of Carl, and wishing futilely that things could have been different between them. When the men joined them later beside the pool for a drink, Morgan could not prevent herself from envying the Larkans. There was that something special between them that stemmed from their complete trust in each other, and one had only to look at them to know that they loved each other to the exclusion almost of all else.

An intense sadness swept through Morgan, but she was not given much time to brood as the weekend progressed, and she was grateful to Richard Kelly for giving her this brief opportunity to get her life into perspective once more. She had neglected her friends over the past months while she had lived in a fool's paradise, but it was not going to happen again.

'Please keep in touch,' was the last thing Sandra said to Morgan before they returned to Johannesburg on the Sunday afternoon.

Morgan would have liked nothing better than to retain Sandra Larkan's friendship, but she suspected

that Sandra still nurtured the secret hope that something might develop between Richard Kelly and herself, and for that reason alone Morgan decided it would
be advisable to maintain a low profile.

'It was kind of you to invite me here to your home
this weekend, and it was a privilege to meet Graham
and Sandra,' Morgan told Richard as he accompanied
her out to her car.

'I'm pleased you decided to come,' he smiled,
dumping her suitcase on to the back seat, and taking
her hand. 'You were company for Sandra, and more
than made up for the times Graham and I neglected her.'

'See you at the office tomorrow,' she smiled, prising
her hand carefully from his, and a few moments later
she was driving through the gates of his home, and
heading towards the centre of the city.

It was only when Morgan was alone in her flat that
evening that she realised how much it had helped to
have people around her during the past two days. The
emptiness and loneliness of her flat depressed her for
the first time in all the years she had lived alone in
Pretoria, and her thoughts turned inevitably towards
Carl. Her attempts to thrust him from her mind on
this occasion were unsuccessful, and that night she cried
herself to sleep for the second time in a little over a week.

Morgan had plugged out her telephone at the flat,
but she could not do the same at the office, and when
it rang shrilly on her desk three days later, she had no
way of knowing that it would be Carl until she heard
his deep, oddly brusque voice at the other end.

'About this coming weekend, Morgan,' he began
without preamble, and she felt her insides coiling
themselves into a tight knot.

'I'm afraid I won't be here,' she lied desperately, and she was grateful that he could not see the guilt staining her cheeks.

'I have to talk to you.'

'You're talking to me now,' she replied stubbornly, and she could almost feel his anger vibrating across the line all the way from Rossmere to Pretoria.

'I can't say the things I want to say on the telephone.'

'In that case I can only presume that what you have to say isn't important.'

There was an explosive silence that sent a shiver of apprehension up her spine, then he demanded harshly, 'What's got into you, Morgan?'

'Nothing,' she snapped nervously.

'Will you explain to me, then, why you're making it so damn difficult for me to see you or speak to you?'

She sighed inwardly and realised at last that being evasive never really served a purpose, but Carl was being particularly tiresome in thinking he could continue making a fool of her.

'I don't want to see you or speak to you again,' she told him coolly.

'Why not?' he had the gall to enquire, and it made her anger rise like those swift summer storms on the reef. What kind of idiot did this arrogant, egotistical man think she was?

'You know the answer to that question better than I do,' she told him icily, and slammed the receiver down on to its cradle with a force which she hoped would jolt him at the other end.

'Condemned, convicted and sentenced,' an accusing voice remarked softly, and she looked up sharply to find Richard observing her from the communicating door with a wry smile hovering about his lips.

'I think I can safely say that I know Carl Ziegler better than you do,' she replied furiously, her hands shaking so much that she hid them in her lap and clenched them tightly.

'Perhaps,' Richard conceded with an infuriating calmness, 'but even the most hardened criminal is entitled to a hearing.'

He had entered his office and had closed the door behind him before she had time to think of a reply, but later, when she had calmed down sufficiently to think rationally, she was forced to admit that there was some truth in what Richard had said. She had condemned, convicted, and sentenced Carl without a hearing, but what would be the purpose of such a hearing when she knew that it would only prolong and intensify the agony of loving a man with whom there was no future?

Morgan fed a sheet of paper into the typewriter, absently typed a few words, and pulled a face when she realised she had made a mistake. She ripped out the paper, tore it to shreds before she dropped it into the wastepaper basket, and tried again. She would have to concentrate on what she was doing, or she might find herself working late that evening to complete the brief Richard was waiting for.

The afternoon somehow progressed without further mishaps, and when she arrived at her flat she kept herself busy washing her hair and making herself something to eat. With nothing left to do eventually, she picked up a book and tried to read, but instead she found herself thinking of the conversation she had had with Carl that afternoon. Perhaps she should have agreed to see him, but then again, what purpose would it have served? He could be very persuasive, and she did not want to believe in him again only to be disillusioned. She tried to thrust these thoughts from her mind to concentrate on her book, but she felt angry and guilty at the same time and, exasperated, she finally flung the book aside and went to bed.

Morgan was still awake at nine-thirty when someone rang her doorbell insistently. Not bothering to put anything on her feet, she pulled on her silk dressing gown and went to answer it. It could only be the caretaker, she decided. It was his habit to call on each resident occasionally to enquire whether everything was in order, but Morgan had to admit that he had left it a bit late on that particular evening.

'Is that you, Mr Olivier?' she asked moments later, opening the door a fraction, but her heart almost stopped beating when she recognised her late visitor. It was Carl, and the expression on his face was sufficient to send a chill of fear through her when he thrust his way into the flat and closed the door firmly behind him. 'How dare you force your way in here without an invitation?' she demanded at once, hiding her feelings behind a display of anger.

He brushed past her without speaking and, before she could guess what he intended doing, he strode into the lounge, and moments later she saw the unplugged cord of the telephone swinging from his hand.

'So this is why there's never a reply when I try to get through to you in the evenings,' he remarked harshly, his eyes narrowed slits of blue fire as he flung the cord to the floor and turned to face her accusingly.

'If I choose to unplug my telephone then it's no

business of yours.' Her chin lifted defiantly. 'What do you want?'

'You and I are going to have a talk,' he replied gratingly, taking her arm in a painful grip and marching her roughly across the room.

'Let me go!' she snapped furiously, trying to break free, but his fingers merely tightened like a vice about her arm, and she had to bite down hard on her lip to prevent herself from crying out.

'Sit down!' Carl barked, thrusting her so violently into one of the chairs that it almost tipped backwards in the process.

'Your behaviour is loathsome!' she accused, anger sparking from her eyes.

'*Shut up!*' The savagery in his voice made her recoil inwardly from him as he stood towering over her, and something warned her that she would regret it if she tried to escape from him. 'The last time I saw you everything was still pretty hunky-dory between us,' he lashed her verbally, 'and I think I'm entitled to know what happened between *then* and *now* that you should want to avoid me as if I've got some kind of infectious disease!'

Morgan looked away from those narrowed, probing eyes which usually saw too much, and decided that, if he could put on an innocent act, then so could she. 'I don't know what you're talking about.'

He leaned over her, his hands on the arms of her chair imprisoning her, and his face so close to her own that she could see the pores in his skin. 'Don't play dumb with me, baby, because I know you're not,' he warned in a dangerously quiet voice that succeeded in driving the colour from her cheeks. 'You owe me an explanation, and I'm not going to leave here until I get a satisfactory answer.'

He meant it, she could see that, and, swallowing convulsively, she asked nervously, 'What exactly do you want to know?'

'Why am I being given the brush-off?' he demanded, straightening and moving a little away from her to lean against the wall beside the hi-fi.

Her throat ached and her pulses were drumming against her temples while she tried desperately to regain her composure, but that was rather difficult when she was so embarrassingly aware of those incredibly blue eyes surveying her with a certain insolence from head to toe until her body felt heated beneath the silk of her robe.

She stared fixedly at the small shaggy carpet beneath her bare feet and, taking a deep breath, finally said with icy calmness, 'I think you'll understand when I tell you that I happened to see you with Gloria De La Rey.'

During the ensuing silence she looked up to see the blankness of his expression replaced by dawning comprehension, then his eyes narrowed to angry slits once more.

'I get it!' he muttered through his teeth. 'You managed to leave your office early after all, and arrived at the hotel that evening to see me leaving with said lady, but you didn't think to go inside and make enquiries, did you? If you had, then you would have been given the note I left for you with the desk clerk, and that note would have explained everything.'

'What was there to explain?' she demanded scathingly. 'That you were having an affair with her because you found her more accommodating in that category while you were negotiating on a business level with her husband?'

Carl went white about the mouth. 'So I'm still the big bad wolf, am I?'

'Was there ever a time when you were not?'

He pushed himself away from the wall to tower over her once more, and her insides quaked nervously when she saw his hands clench and unclench themselves at his sides as if he were contemplating putting them around her throat.

'For your information, madam,' he explained with heavy sarcasm, and a glittering hardness in his eyes that changed his appearance so totally she almost wanted to weep, 'the lady in question was supposed to have dined at the hotel that evening with friends, but before her friends arrived she received a telephone call to inform her that her husband had been involved in an accident out at the steel plant. I happened to be in the foyer at the time, and I realised that the lady was too distraught to drive herself to the hospital. I introduced myself and, in distress as she was, she accepted my offer to take her to her husband—whom, by the way, I have not had the privilege of meeting. I waited for her at the hospital until she had assured herself that he was no longer in danger, then I drove her back to the hotel. I followed her to her home at a discreet distance, just to make sure that she arrived safely, and after that I returned to the hotel. I was told that you hadn't called to pick up my note, and naturally assumed you hadn't managed to come, then I went to bed—*alone!*'

He paused as if expecting her to say something, then

his mouth twisted with a cynicism that sliced deep. 'As for the accusation that I'm negotiating a business deal with her husband . . . well, there's no truth in that at all, and you may check that out if you wish. I hope that my explanation satisfies you, but if there's still some doubt in your mind, then I suggest you telephone the hotel and speak to the chap at the reception desk. He should still recall vividly the incidents that evening while I stood around in the foyer hoping you could make it.'

'That won't be necessary,' she said unsteadily, her colour coming and going with regret, guilt, and several other emotions which built up to a pitch to leave her feeling disgusted with herself. 'Condemned, convicted, and sentenced,' Richard's accusation rang in her ears, and she felt like crawling into the nearest hole to hide herself in shame.

'Don't tell me, Morgan,' Carl demanded derisively, 'that you're going to accept the word of a scoundrel like me?'

Her cheeks were burning when she got to her feet and turned blindly from the scornful accusation in his eyes. 'Gloria De La Rey is Richard Kelly's client. We knew that she was having an affair with someone, and when we——'

'*We?*' Carl interrupted sharply.

'My car was in the garage for a repair job, so Richard gave me a lift to the hotel that evening,' she explained hurriedly.

'Go on,' Carl prompted after a momentary pause. 'You were saying that you knew she was having an affair with someone.'

'Y-yes,' she heard herself stammering like an idiot. 'When we saw you together, I—we——'

'You thought I was that guy,' he filled in for her harshly.

She gestured helplessly with her hands, and turned to face him. 'I'm sorry,' she murmured lamely.

'*You're sorry!*' he repeated savagely, advancing upon her and shaking her by the shoulders until she was afraid her neck would snap. 'I've gone nearly out of my mind this past week wondering what I'd done to deserve the cold shoulder, and all you can say is you're *sorry!*'

'What—What else can I say?' she asked haltingly, fighting frantically against the tears that threatened to spill from her lashes.

'I can think of quite a few things you could say, but I'm damned if I'm going to prompt you!' shouted Carl, thrusting her away from him with a force that sent her staggering back against a chair, and she was still trying to regain her balance when he let himself out of her flat and slammed the door behind him.

She felt the vibration of it beneath her feet, and for several dazed seconds she stood there staring blankly at nothing in particular then she collapsed into the chair and buried her face in her trembling hands. She tried desperately to hold the tears in check, but she couldn't, and they trickled through her fingers while she wept long and silently, cursing herself for her stupidity.

Morgan had never thought Carl capable of such terrible anger, but she had judged him without sufficient evidence, as Richard had warned, and Carl had had every right to be angry with her. His error was perhaps understandable under the circumstances. Everything had seemed to fit so perfectly; knowing

Carl and being aware of the details of Gloria's divorce, but that was no excuse, and it did not prevent Morgan from feeling more than just a little sick inside.

It was over, she thought miserably. Why she should feel at all hurt about it, she could not say. This was what she had wanted; a nice clean break in their relationship, and that was exactly what she had got. *It was over*. She would think about it again in the morning, she would *feel* again tomorrow, but right that minute all she wanted was to crawl into bed and, she hoped, never wake up again.

Falling asleep was not so easy when her mind was in a painful turmoil, and her eyelids swollen with tears which continued to flow despite her efforts to control them. Exhaustion finally took its toll, and she went to sleep with her hot face buried in her damp pillow, but Carl's angry face haunted her even in her sleep.

CHAPTER TEN

Morgan sat heavy-eyed, pale and listless behind her desk the following morning when Richard arrived at the office, and one glance in her direction was enough to make him pause abruptly beside her desk.

'You don't look so well this morning,' he announced, eyeing her curiously.

There was no sense in hiding the truth from him, so she said tiredly, 'I saw Carl last night.'

'And he told you that, on a certain Friday evening not so long ago, he gave my client a lift to the hospital to see her husband because she was in no fit state to drive herself.'

Her head shot up and her eyes widened with incredulous surprise. 'How did you know that?'

'I had a lengthy discussion with Gloria De La Rey and her husband last night,' he explained with a tolerant smile, 'and you will be happy to know that they've decided to patch up their differences.'

If Morgan had wanted proof, then here it was, and self-disgust rose like a wave of nausea within her. 'I think I'm going to be sick.'

'I thought you'd be pleased to know that they are attempting to save their marriage,' Richard remarked with a puzzled look on his rugged face.

'I *am* pleased for Mrs De La Rey's sake, but when I think of what I—I accused Carl of, I could——'

'Kick yourself?' he questioned with a wry smile when she paused abruptly.

'Something like that,' she nodded unhappily. 'And Carl, of course, was very angry.'

'He had every right to be.'

She winced inwardly. 'Don't rub it in, will you?'

'I gather you didn't straighten out this misunderstanding afterwards?' he asked shrewdly, studying her closely, and she shook her head.

'He was too furious with me, and I doubt if I'll see him again, but ... perhaps it's best that it happened this way.'

Richard stared at her for interminable seconds, then he shook his head in a perplexed fashion and turned away. 'I don't think I'll ever understand women!'

Morgan smiled wanly, but did not comment on his statement, and a few minutes later he buzzed her to come in and take dictation.

The remainder of the week passed with comparative ease, and so did the weekend, but her heart felt like a painful piece of lead in her breast, and she seldom slept through one night without waking and thinking of Carl. She was not a child, she cautioned herself often whenever the tears threatened. She was an adult, and she was going to be sensible about the whole thing. There was no such thing as a broken heart; that was simply a lot of romantic rubbish. She had existed perfectly without Carl before, and she could do so again. The positive approach always worked, she tried to convince herself, and it *did*, but only up to a point. There was nothing positive, however, in the way she felt when, on the Wednesday of the following week, the ringing of the telephone awakened her in the middle of the night.

She stumbled out of bed and groped wildly for the

light switch. Her eyes, heavy with sleep and narrowed against the brightness of the light, focused in dismay on the alarm clock beside her bed. *Twelve-forty-five!*

'Who on earth could be calling at this time of the night?' she muttered to herself, agitatedly brushing her hair out of her face as she staggered out of the bedroom and into the lounge to answer the telephone, but a few moments later she was surprised at herself for not having guessed that there was only one person who was mad enough to call her up at that time of the night.

'May I come and see you, Morgan?' Carl's deep voice made her heart behave like a wild bird fluttering wildly against the bars of its cage.

'Do you realise that it's almost one o'clock in the morning?' she demanded incredulously.

'I know, honey, and I apologise, but there's something important I have to discuss with you, and it can't wait.'

'But surely it——'

'I'll be there in a few minutes,' he interrupted her protests, and the next instant she was left holding the receiver with the dialling tone purring in her ear.

She dropped the receiver back on to its cradle and stood for a moment as if she was not quite sure what to do, then she fled into her bedroom and dressed herself hastily in slacks and a cotton blouse. She washed the sleep out of her eyes, applied a little powder and lipstick to her face, and brushed the tangles out of her hair. She was still fiddling around with her hair when the doorbell rang, and sheer nervousness made the brush slip from her fingers to fall on the carpeted floor with a thud which she hoped had not awakened the people in the flat below her.

Her insides were shaking when she hurried towards the door and uttered the precautionary, 'Who is it?'

'It's Carl,' his deep, familiar voice reached her ears. 'Open up, will you?'

Her fingers fumbled nervously as she lifted the latch, and her heart was beating suffocatingly fast when the door swung open to admit Carl. His presence, as always, made her feel a little shaky in the knees and, angry with herself for being so weak, she said sharply, 'You're *crazy*, coming here at this time of the night!'

'We have to talk, Morgan,' he said, following her into the lounge.

'I thought we'd said all there was to say the other night.'

'Not quite.'

'You look terrible,' she told him, noticing the greyness of his pallor and the grimness of his expression when she finally allowed herself to take a long, hard look at him.

'It's been a hectic day,' he smiled faintly.

'And a hectic evening, no doubt,' she added drily when her sensitive nose picked up the scent of cigar smoke and whisky.

'Yeah, you can say that again,' he grunted, taking off his jacket and tie, and flinging them on to a chair. 'I would have been here earlier if I hadn't had to wait for a call from my office in Washington.'

Tiredness had etched deep lines into his attractive face, and her heart melted with tenderness, despite her efforts to the contrary.

'I suppose you could do with a cup of coffee.'

'Later!' His fingers latched on to her wrist, and his touch sent that familiar current of awareness surging through her. 'I've got to say what's on my mind first.'

'It must be important if it couldn't wait for a more opportune moment,' she said, unable to keep that hint of sarcasm out of her voice, but he seemed not to hear it.

'We had a board meeting this rnoon, and everyone's in favour of the Triton being incorporated into my company in the United States. I'm returning to the States in a little more than two weeks to finalise everything.' Her heart lurched painfully and, when she said nothing, he frowned down at her. 'You don't seem surprised.'

She pulled her wrist free of his light clasp and, for her own comfort, she circled a chair so that it stood directly between them. 'There were rumours to that effect, and rumours have a way of circulating.'

Carl accepted that without comment as he lowered himself tiredly on to the sofa and stretched his long legs out before him. 'Your father has been elected to take over as managing director of the Triton.'

'I see,' Morgan murmured noncommittally, wondering what her father thought of the whole thing, and she smothered a smile when she recalled their conversation in connection with this matter.

'Morgan, honey . . .' Carl was on his feet again, a restless, almost agitated look about him which she could not fully understand. 'Come to the States with me?'

She was, at first, too stunned to grasp what he was asking of her, but when she had recovered sufficiently, she snapped cynically, 'As what, may I ask? As your mistress?'

'As my *wife*.'

Her breath locked in her throat, and she felt

momentarily winded as she stood there staring up at him. She had to be dreaming, or perhaps she was going mad, but, either way, she was not going to have her hopes raised for the sake of a mirage.

'Don't be ridiculous!' she croaked cynically. 'Marriage isn't your style. You told me so yourself, remember?'

Carl gestured angrily with his hands. 'That was a crazy thing to say, and I know it!'

'You're even crazier if you think I don't realise that you're offering me marriage simply because your ego has been busted,' she accused hoarsely. 'You've always been able to get any woman you wanted, but you failed with me, and now your only solution to the problem is *marriage*!'

He took a step towards her. 'Listen to me, Morgan.'

'No, *you* listen to *me*! In a year or two, perhaps even sooner, you'll have grown tired of me, and what happens then?' Her legs were shaking so much beneath her that she had to clutch at the back of the chair for support as she continued scathingly, 'Does our—marriage—end in divorce? Or do you simply go ahead and have your little affairs, while I have to sit at home and be satisfied with those inbetween moments when you have no one better in your sights? Is that what you have in mind for me?'

If she had not been so concerned with the agonised confusion of her own disposition, she might have noticed the danger signals in those narrowed eyes observing her so intently, but she was blind to everything at that moment except the aching despair that made her writhe inwardly.

'It's not like that at all!' Carl contradicted her harshly.

'Isn't it?' she mocked him now.

'*No, damn you, it isn't!*'

He picked up the chair that stood between them and flung it aside with a total disregard for the people in the flat below. He had moved so quickly that there had been no time for her to back away, and she was lifted high in his arms as if she weighed no more than a feather to him.

'Put me down!' she begged frantically, fear drumming against her temples when she realised that he was carrying her into the bedroom. 'Carl . . . *please!*'

Her struggles were futile, and he was beyond hearing her pleas. His eyes were hard, and his jaw unrelenting. There was no escape, and Morgan was horrifyingly aware of this when he dropped her unceremoniously on to the bed and held her captive there with his hard body. He had made use of sensual persuasion before, but on this occasion his mouth bruised hers cruelly into submission, and his hands on her body were merciless in their demand.

Caught between fear and a terrible longing, she was too much to resist, and the raging torrent of his passion swept over her until she felt as though she were drowning in it. His angry desire was a flame that seared her to her soul, but while her body quivered beneath his with an aching need, her mind was filled with cold rejection. This was lust, not love, and she tasted the salt of her own tears in her mouth when his lips found hers once more.

'Oh, my God, what am I doing!' he groaned at length, and through her tears she saw his features distorted with self-derision. With gentle fingers he brushed the dampness from her cheeks, then he lowered his head and kissed away the teardrops which still clung to her lashes. 'Don't cry, Morgan,' he murmured thickly. 'I want you, but not like this. I know you're convinced that I'm the worst cad to ever walk this earth, but I beg you to believe that I've never wanted to do anything to hurt you.'

The tears continued to flow, she could not stop them, and he moved away from her abruptly to sit on the edge of the bed with his elbows resting on his knees and his head in his hands. She had never seen him look so utterly dejected before, and she knew then that, no matter what, she could not bear to see him that way.

'Carl . . .' she began haltingly, not quite sure what to say or do as she raised herself up on one elbow.

'I don't really deserve the reputation I've been saddled with,' he confessed, seemingly unaware that she had spoken. 'There've been plenty of women in my life, I admit that, but very few of them were serious affairs. I've been too busy most of my life getting my business off the ground, and marriage was out simply because I never thought I would ever meet a woman whom I could feel so strongly about that I would want to spend the rest of my life with her.' He turned towards her then, and his grim, tortured expression tore at her heart. 'I don't want an affair with you, honey. I want to *marry* you. I want to make a total commitment, and I want to swear before all that's holy that I shall love and cherish you for the rest of my life.'

The most incredible joy, piercingly sweet in its intensity, surged through her and, with a heart too full to speak, she held out her arms to him. Carl stared at her for a moment with a touching uncertainty mirrored in his eyes, then he came into her arms and buried his face against her throat. They clung to each other fiercely, almost as if they were afraid to let go, and his whispered words of love fed her hungry heart until she felt quite delirious with happiness.

'Do you think you could tolerate me for the rest of your life?' he asked eventually when he raised his head to look down into luminous grey-green eyes that no longer hid her feelings.

'For the rest of my life, and beyond,' she whispered huskily, running her fingers through his short fair hair, and loving the feel of its softness beneath her fingers. 'I love you, Carl. You must have guessed that a long time ago, and that's why I was so afraid to continue our relationship. I didn't think you could ever love me . . . *really* love me, I mean.'

An odd little smile touched his mouth and dispersed with some of the grimness. 'That letter you found was my sister's reply to a letter in which I'd told her that I'd at last met my fate. If you'd read it you would have known long ago.'

'You loved me then already?' Morgan asked incredulously.

'I was lost that first day when I called on your father and found you sleeping on the terrace,' he laughed softly against her throat. 'I thought then that I'd never seen anything quite so lovely, and I knew that I had to have you. At first it was simply a case of wanting you, but it didn't take me long to discover that what I really wanted was a lifetime affair, and this last trip to the United States really clinched it for me.'

His mouth found hers and he kissed her with a renewed hunger as if those days and nights away from her was a memory he wished to erase permanently from his mind.

'That letter you wrote to me ...' Morgan began when she was allowed to catch her breath.

'I'd played up the bad guy bit so long that I was afraid you wouldn't believe me if I came right out with it and told you that I loved you, so I tried to tell you in some other way how much you meant to me, and how much I needed you.' Those deceptively lazy eyes met hers quizzically. 'Didn't the message come across that way?'

'It came across loud and clear,' she sighed tremulously, 'but I was too scared to accept it at face value, and then, when I saw you coming out of the hotel with Gloria De La Rey, I decided that it was just as well that I didn't read too much into your letter.'

'Trust me, honey,' Carl said thickly, brushing a silky strand of hair away from her flushed cheek. 'I give you my solemn promise here and now that I'll never purposely let you down in any way.'

She had never seen such a wonderful mixture of love, tenderness and passion in a man's eyes before. It almost succeeded in taking her breath away, and it felt as if her heart wanted to burst with happiness.

'Oh, Carl!' she whispered ecstatically, flinging her arms about his neck and pressing closer to him. 'Hold me ... hold me, please, and help me to believe that this isn't a dream.'

He held her close against his hard body and kissed her tenderly at first, but passion flared between them, and the buttons down the front of her blouse gave way beneath his fingers to pave the way for his seeking mouth as it roamed the curve of her taut breast. A shudder of desire coursed through her, and her hands ached to touch him as he was touching her. She tugged impatiently at the buttons of his shirt and slid her hands across the hair-roughened wall of his chest towards the smoothness of his wide shoulders. The muscles rippled beneath her untutored fingers as she caressed him eagerly, and it was only when she felt him shudder against her that she realised what she was doing.

'Morgan darling,' Carl cautioned hoarsely, 'don't be so sweet and willing in my arms. I want you so much at this moment, and you're not making it easy for me to behave myself.'

With every nerve and sinew still throbbing with desire, she escaped from his arms and fumbled the buttons of her blouse into place. 'I—I'd better make a fresh pot of coffee, and then you really must go.'

His eyes followed her from the room, and it felt oddly as if she were walking on air. *He loves me,* her heart kept singing, and it was almost too incredibly wonderful to believe.

Carl came up behind her in the kitchen, his strong arms circling her slim waist while she set out the cups and waited for the coffee to percolate. 'I can't bear to be away from you for even a minute,' he said with his lips against her hair. 'I don't suppose there's any chance of your coming back to Rossmere with me, is there?'

'No chance at all,' she confirmed, a smile on her lips as she turned in his arms and linked her hands behind his silvery head, then her expression sobered. 'Are you really going straight back to Rossmere from here?'

'I have to be at the office at eight tomorrow morning,' he said, kissing the tip of her small, straight nose.

'But you can't put in a full day's work when you haven't slept a wink all night,' she protested, concern clouding her eyes.

'I'll manage,' he grinned down at her.

'But you——'

His lips silenced hers in a long, satisfying kiss, and she lost herself in his embrace until the bubbling of the percolator brought her to her senses.

'I suggest you wait in the lounge while I pour the coffee,' she suggested a little breathlessly, wriggling out of his arms, and he obeyed her with a certain amount of reluctance.

It was two-thirty in the morning when they finally placed their empty cups in the tray, and Morgan lapsed into a contemplative silence where she sat beside Carl on the sofa. She dreaded to think what the neighbours would say if they should hear of her midnight caller, but most of all she dreaded the thought of having to confront her father with the news that she was going to marry Carl.

'A penny for your thoughts?' Carl asked eventually, sliding an arm about her shoulders, and raising her hand to his lips.

'I was wondering what my father will have to say when he hears about us,' she replied without hesitation, and her teeth nibbled absently at her bottom lip.

'Your father knows already.'

Her eyes were a little bewildered when they met his. 'He knows?'

'I've formally asked his permission to propose marriage to his daughter,' Carl smiled, drawing her wholly into his arms. 'That was one of the reasons why I was so late in getting here this evening.'

'Oh, my gosh!' she exclaimed anxiously into his shoulder. 'What did he say?'

'He gave me his permission to ask you to marry me, but he also said he hoped you'd refuse me.'

'Did he honestly say that?' Morgan asked nervously, not quite sure whether Carl was being serious, or simply teasing her.

'He said he wasn't at all in favour of his daughter becoming the boss's wife, but if that was what you wanted, then he'd give us his unstinted blessing,' Carl smiled broadly, allaying some of her fears. 'He was in a pretty good mood, I must say.'

There were so many questions that still needed answering, but Carl's mouth got in the way, and for several heart-stopping seconds she was subjected to a display of passion that left her trembling in his arms with a desire that was becoming achingly familiar.

'Do you think you could be ready to marry me before I have to leave for the States?' he asked against her throat.

She tried to ignore the sensual touch of his fingers through the cotton at her breast while she did a swift mental calculation. 'A little over two weeks is rather short notice, but I dare say I'll manage.'

'Will you mind living in the States?' the inevitable question was asked and, drawing his face out into the open, Morgan allowed him to see into her very soul where no further doubts lurked.

'I don't mind where we live. All I want is to be with you.'

She felt his muscled chest heave against her, and a tender triumph flickered in his eyes as he crushed her against him with a fierceness which threatened to crack her ribs.

'Sweetheart, I love you,' he grunted, and a barrage of kisses followed that left her feeling weak with joy and intense happiness.

'If you don't go now you'll still be here when the sun comes up,' she finally warned him unsteadily.

'When will I see you again?' he demanded when she had somehow managed to get him to the door.

'I'll drive up to Rossmere for the weekend,' she promised.

'I'll be counting the hours!'

She was caught up in a swift embrace, then Carl kissed her hard on the mouth, and left her feeling dazed, but happy.

The time passed swiftly and happily for Morgan. Richard Kelly accepted her resignation quite happily, and her father appeared to be pleased about her coming marriage to Carl, but she somehow sensed a hidden anxiety. Carl had made plans for them to spend a few days at a holiday resort along the Vaal river before they flew to New York, and Morgan was far too busy training Richard's new private secretary to feel at all jittery about her marriage to Carl which was so close to becoming a reality.

On her wedding day, however, when she was alone with her father for a few moments before they were to be driven to the church, he voiced his uncertainty for the first time.

'Are you sure this is what you want, Morgan?' he asked.

'I've never been more sure of anything in all my life,' she replied without the slightest hesitation, and Andrew's features relaxed as he nodded briefly.

'That's all I wanted to know,' he smiled at her, and after that Morgan had no time to brood over their hurried conversation. Their car was waiting, and so was Carl.

That night, when she stood in the circle of her husband's arms in their hotel room, she recalled her father's uncertainty, and she almost wished he could have been there to see the expression on Carl's face at that moment. He was looking at her with such infinite tenderness in his eyes that it almost brought a lump to her throat, and his hands were shaking with the extent of his feelings as they made their way through the silken mass of her titian-coloured hair.

'It feels as if I've been waiting a lifetime for this moment,' he said, his deep voice vibrating with emotion.

'Poor darling,' she teased gently, slipping her arms about his waist and resting her head against his broad chest where she could hear the quick, heavy beat of his heart. 'Has the waiting been so terrible?'

'It's been rather wearing on the nerves,' he confessed with a smile in his voice. 'There's so much I want to show you and share with you in the States, and . . .' He raised her face to his, and suddenly everything else was forgotten. 'Do you trust me?'

'Implicitly,' she confessed without hesitation as he lifted her in his arms and deposited her gently on the bed.

He switched off the bedside lamp, bathing the room in moonlight, then she felt his lips against her hair, her forehead, her eyes, and her cheeks, and when at last he parted her eager, waiting lips, she knew that she was half way to a paradise where only he could take her. She was trapped in the silken web of Carl's love, and she no longer had any need or desire to escape.

Harlequin® Plus

A WORD ABOUT THE AUTHOR

Yvonne Whittal grew up in South Africa, spending her summers on the coast and her winter months inland at a sheep farm in the Karoo region. It was there that Yvonne came to know the farmers who loved the earth and faced a never ending struggle for survival. Her first novel, *East to Barryvale* (Romance #1915, published in 1975), was inspired by the people of the area.

Yvonne began scribbling stories at a very early age, and in her teens she considered writing as a profession. But marriage and three daughters caused her to shelve that idea...for a while.

Then, rusty after so many years away from her writing, Yvonne enrolled in a fiction-writing course and set to work. She began with short stories and moved on to a novel, which took several months to complete. "Fortunately," she laughingly comments on her slow start, "I did not have to make a living out of my writing then. Otherwise, I would surely have starved!"

❀❀ FREE ❀❀
*Harlequin Reader Service Catalog**

A complete listing of all titles currently available in
Harlequin Romance, Harlequin Presents,
Classic Library and Superromance.

**Special offers
and exciting
new books, too!**

*Catalog varies each month.

**Complete and mail
this coupon today!**
